Seven Hills One Light

a novel of
Ancient Rome

Book one: In the Shadow of Lions

HAZEL DAINS

WEATHERED & WELL
press

WEATHERED & WELL PRESS
Published in Ontario, Canada

Content Disclaimer
This novel explores themes of Christian faith, persecution, and moral challenges in ancient Rome. If you're interested in stories that delve into personal beliefs and the struggle to hold onto them in the face of adversity, you'll find much to reflect on.

Hardcover ISBN: 978-1-998319-39-8

WEATHERED & WELL
press

Grab your

#FREE

digital sneak peak into Hazel's work-in-progress

HEARTS aglow

By claiming your free digital sneak peek of "Hearts Aglow," you are agreeing to sign up for Hazel Dains' monthly newsletter. As a subscriber, you'll receive exclusive new release details, opportunities to join my street team, coupons and discounts, plus additional freebies and special offers

Stay connected and be the first to experience everything Hazel Dains has to offer!

Table of Contents

Maßstab 1:54.000
0   500   1000
Meter.

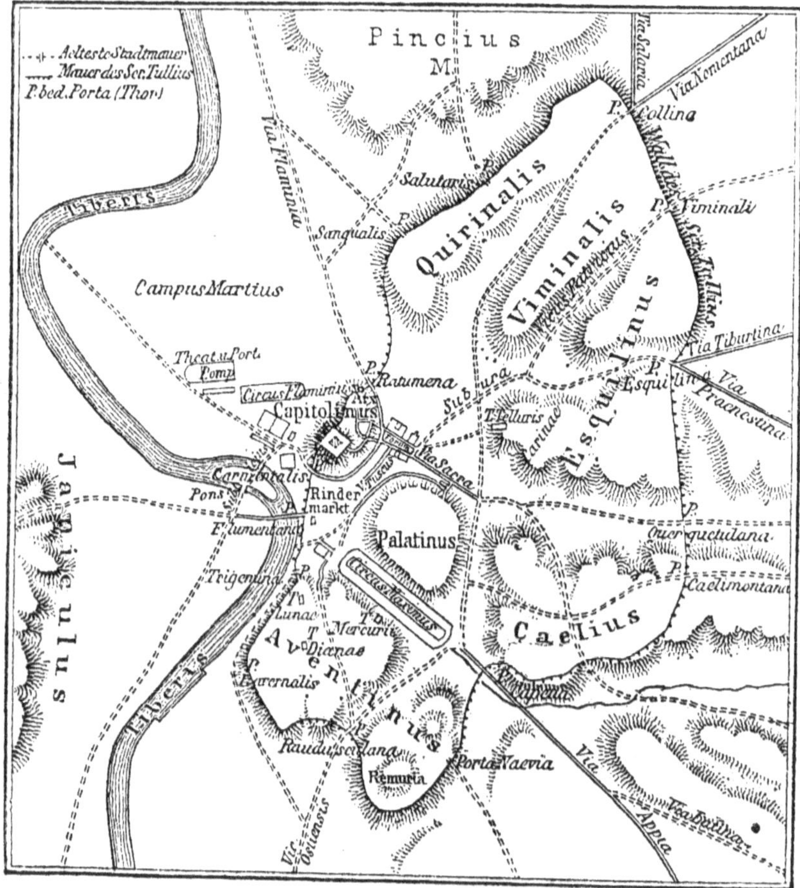
Aelteste Stadtmauer
Mauer des Ser. Tullius
P. bed. Porta (Thor)
Pincius M.
Via Salaria
Via Nomentana
P. Collina
Quirinalis
Viminalis
P. Viminali
Via Flaminia
Salutaris
Sanqualis
Campus Martius
Vicus Patricius
Agger Ser. Tullii
Via Tiburtina
Esquilinus
P. Esquilin
P. Via
Praenestina
Theat. u. Port. Pomp.
Tiberis
Circus Flaminius
P. Ratumena
Subura
Arx
Capitolinus
T. Telluris
Carinae
Via Sacra
V. Tuscus
Carmentalis
Pons
Rinder markt
Via Ostiensis
P. Flumentana
Palatinus
Circus Maximus
Querquetulana
P.
Caelimontana
Trigemina
P.
T. Lunae
T. Mercuri
T. Dianae
Caelius
Aventinus
P. Lavernalis
Via Appia
Porta Naevia
Raudusculana
Remuria
Janiculus
Tiberis

"Greet those workers in the
Lord, Tryphaena and
Tryphosa."

Romans 16:12

chapter one
ON DISPLAY

There was nothing she could do but stand there, a silent witness as two members of the urban cohort dragged a man down Vicus Canarius on a slave's rope. Knit within the masses, Tryphosa stood as still as she could, even as the breath of the person behind her tickled the back of her graceful neck. Her mosey eyes squinted as a ray of the setting sun blocked her view of the progression. She looked to her right where her tall and slender sister stood, beautiful and adorned in her only remaining blue silk stola, her long golden hair gathered together at the nap of her neck. Her sister's eyes darted from one captive to the next as they were ceremoniously paraded along the strata before them. Then Phosa knew. She's looking for someone.

And then a pair of agonized brown eyes met hers. And at once, she knew him. Festus. Tears streamed down her face as she remembered his sweet, simple smile that was now replaced by a sorrowful cry for help. Phosa couldn't hold back her tears as she looked away from the prisoner, unable to handle the overwhelming grief in his eyes. On every side, Phosa was walled in by jeering Romans, badgering the centurians to bring out more traitors. She dared not look them in the eyes. "They get what they deserve, the lot of them!" A short, older woman growled coarsely from behind her.

Phosa remained still and silent, unable to resist the urge to eavesdrop. "What did they do?" the man beside her asked, innocently enough.

"Oh, *stultissime!* Don't you know? These are the Christ followers. The ones who have denied the gods and brought wrath upon Rome!"

"Oh surely you don't believe they're all to blame. I've never met no Christian that murdered his mother."

"Hush! Or the very man you speak of will send you to the lions!"

Tryphosa felt her heart thumping in her chest, faster and faster, until all the world around her was a haze. The crowd's incessant jeers faded into a distant moan. And she was alone, gripped by fear. She was tied up. Tightly. Someone was placing something over her shoulders.

"Phosa!" She opened her eyes, and there standing before her was her sister. She looked worried. "Phosa! Head up!"

As Phosa inhaled deeply, she could smell the sweet yet musty scent of burning incense filling the air. Pulling her cream wool shawl around her for comfort. Tryphosa scanned her surroundings, anticipating that she would be the next target. After all, she was part of the Way, and there were countless others like her. Her sister had warned her that this day would come, the day when the *corhortes urabane* put them on display as enemies of Rome. But she wasn't ready.

The streets were crowded with onlookers lining the edge of the *strata* as processions of terrified men and women, and even children, made their way towards their impending death.

Every instinct in her body told her to run, to disappear into the thick crowds and get out of the city before they find her, too. But resolve kept her there like a statue. If she left the parade now, people would talk. And worse, the steps of the *corhortes* would follow her. Attendance at this spectacle was mandatory for every citizen of Rome. Justice had to be served and respected. Without justice, the gods would not smile upon Rome. But none of that mattered to Tryphosa anymore. She felt a gentle tug on her shawl and noticed her sister's eyes were fixed on her. *That's the sign that we can go. Good.* She was about to turn her back and make her way through the rowdy crowd, filled with jeers and shouts aimed at the condemned. But before she could move, she felt a hand on her shoulder.

"Hey, you!"

Unconsciously, she spun around to confront whoever had stopped her. The man towered before her; his pointy nose and jagged brown eyes asked questions she did not want to answer.

"Have you been taught no decency? No respect for the gods?" He grabbed her by the arm. Phosa grimaced in discomfort but fought to suppress any outward reaction, not wanting to draw attention.

"I, uh..." Fear gripped her into silence.

"These people are traitors of Rome. Do your duty, and watch as justice unfolds!"

"Yes, I-"

"Good sir., please Do you dare defy the gods and show mercy to such as these?"

Phena rushed to her side. "My good sir, please remove your hand from my sister's arm. She is merely tired and requires rest."

"Well," The bewildering man loosened his grip on Phosa's arm and said, "It is because of people like her that our great city is rotting!"

Suddenly, the man's lips curled into a snarl as he aimed a glob of spit towards the ground. His angry eyes narrowed as he turned on his heel and stormed away. Phosa breathed again, relieved to see that bulk of a man retreating. But she didn't have long to enjoy her arm's freedom as Phena immediately grabbed it again and pulled her more quickly through the throng of people, their focus on the neverending procession behind them.

"That was close!" Phosa whispered, catching her breath for the first time in a while.

"Hush, you fool!"

They pushed their way through until they reached a shaded tree and patch of grass next to the nearby *circus publicas* stand.

"Hello, ladies." A young man with dark brown hair and hazel eyes greeted them from behind the desk.

"Great day for a parade!" He shouted with a grin.

"Yes, sir!" Phena replied as she rushed past the postal worker's stall, pulling Phosa behind her, her light blue linen dress flowing in the wind. The air was heavy with the scent of dust and sweat, mixed with the aromas of hot food from the nearby *thermopolium* and animals tethered at the side of the street. Phosa's arm was red and marked from where her sister had been grasping her.

"Ok, ok. We're out of the crowd. Let go!"

Phosa pulled her arm from her sister's clutches and rubbed the place where, only seconds ago, her sister had been digging her fingernails into her skin.

"Ouch!"

"Oh, get over it! We have to move faster!" Phena urged as she quickened her pace, forcing Phosa to quicken hers. The setting sun grazed the dusty streets of Rome, golden glow on the buildings and passersby. The occasional horse-drawn cart passed them by, a stench of manure and sweat left in its wake. The usual noise of the city was dimming as the evening progressed, leaving only the noise of coins clanging together and shutters of shop windows coming down in a chorus, signaling the end of a work day. Phena stood in front of her sister, still pulling her along past the *Viale Virgin* and towards *Viale Juniper*.

"Why are you always pulling me around? I can walk, you know!"

"Oh yeah? At the speed of a hermit crab!"

"Where do we need to be? Huh? It's a parade day!"

Fifty years before either of them were born, the Caesars decreed the very first public celebrations and holidays which entitled every freed Roman a day off with free bread, oil, and festivities. Phosa could remember her father taking them to see the processions, where they'd often receive a piece of fresh bread and a cool drink. On days like this, her father would throw her onto his shoulders and make amusing jokes. She felt an ache in her chest, thinking back on those days. The death of her father had left a deep chasm none could fill.

The two women rushed down the street towards their apartment, passing merchant stalls and heavenly-smelling bakeries. Usually, the sound of donkeys braying and heavy carts rattling up and down the cobbled streets of Rome would have been enough to give Phosa a headache, but today, their *strata* was still. They rounded the corner of Canius and Vanae Streets, an intersection that was just a short walk from their apartment block, passing Janis' eatery on the way.

Heaven above! Phosa thought as she caught a whiff of Janis' famous *pinsa Romana* and *Tisana Barrica.*

"Phena! Let's stop! Janis' is open!"

"No, Phena! Rusticus is preparing our meal at home." Rusticus was a good-natured Syrian-born slave that their parents had bought when they were just girls. He'd been a cherished part of their household for years, although he had never chosen to convert to their religion. Despite their differences, there was an undeniable bond between them. Growing up, their home always smelled of the fresh spices of the Orient. When their parents died just a few months before, Rusticus had pledged to stay with them. They walked briskly by Janis' bar and up the steep incline of Esquiline Hill, where there was a hidden staircase that led to the Subura quarter. Phosa was thankful to escape from the noisy and chaotic parade and find solace in a quieter part of town. The taunts and jeers of the crowd were left behind as they entered this more peaceful area. Phosa was just about to step onto the first stair, following closely behind her sister, when a stern Roman voice echoed from somewhere behind her.

"You two!" Phosa instinctively turned and was blinded by the light reflecting off of the centurion's breastplate. When the sun's rays dissipated, she saw a tall and handsome but stern-faced guard wearing a standard long red tunic and leather-bound frilled sublingual. She noticed that the dagger hanging from his belt was dripping with blood.

"What are you doing on these backstreets? Traitors and thieves are still being shown justice!"

"Uuhh, yes, sir. Yes, we…" Phosa stammered in response, her tongue frozen from shock and fear.

"Yes, you have nothing to say? Who are you?"

"We are just two simple sisters of Rome. We have just come from the *Via Victoria* and were watching the criminals...." As always, Phena's tongue worked just fine.

"Had enough then?" The man interjected, seemingly not interested in what Phena had to say. "Why is that, girl? Do you sympathize with the traitors? Perhaps you are traitors yourselves?" The man's face was dark and stern, his eyes cold and calculating as he unsheathed his sharp dagger. Phosa could feel her heart pounding in her chest and her skin prickling with fear as the cold blade of the dagger seemed to inch closer and closer to her. The metallic scent of blood wafted from the dripping dagger, the tang of iron filling Phosa's nose. Phosa could no longer breathe. And words escaped her. *Oh God! This must be the end. Phena! I need you!*

Then, as if on cue, Phosa felt the comfort of her sister's body interfere with the centurion's clearly murderous intent. "Sir, I assure you, there is no need to threaten my sister with a blade," Phena assured him. "We are Roman subjects, simply in need of a respite. A meal. That is all."

The guard's movements were filled with tension and aggression, like a coiled snake ready to strike. But as he turned away, a glimmer of devotion and superstition filled his eyes as he left a tribute for the god of war before continuing on his way,
"Thank you!" Phena calmly shouted after him.
Then unexpectedly, the very air turned to poison as the man's words returned to them, like a slithering venomous serpent, *"ut illius manus, caput, pedes vermes, cancer, vermitudo interet,"* ["May worms, cancer, and decay consume his hands, head, and feet."] And then he was gone.
The sisters hurried away, their hearts thudding in their chests. Phosa felt a shiver run down her spine at the man's threatening words, the image of being led away in chains sending a cold wave of fear through her veins.

"Oh, wow! That was a close one!" Phosa mumbled to herself.

"You almost got us killed! Twice!" Phena complained.

"I'm sorry, sister. I—"

"Phosa! Don't be sorry! Be better! One of these days, I won't be here to get you off the hook!" Phosa knew that her sister was right. But felt like the task was impossible for her. She wasn't nearly as quick-witted as her sister.

They raced to the top of the stairs and then went on their way towards *Clivus Suburanus*. Once they had calmed their breathing and checked for any potential onlookers, they kept walking, stepping over men sleeping off drink from hours before and distant moans of pleasure by men being satisfied in the back alleys. The sisters increased their pace, desperate to avoid being grouped in with the mischief and ruckus that Subura was known for. They finally reached a T in the road and turned right onto *Vicus Patricius*.

Phosa's eyes landed on their apartment block's metal gate, a small source of security and solace in the otherwise impoverished neighborhood. Almost there, almost there. She followed her sister's cues and bent her head down as they passed the open door of the most notorious of public houses, Popina Leonis, known for their sheltering of unregistered prostitutes and other delinquents. Of course, their establishment was in full swing even during a parade. Phosa couldn't resist looking inside and saw two middle-aged men hunched over a rugged wooden pint mug of what was likely cheap wine. One man looked up from his wine and met her eyes.

"Where are you going, girls?" Have something in mind yourselves?" Phosa had no intention of answering and only quickened her pace. Then, to her horror, she heard footsteps behind her.

"Oh, she's running! I love a challenge!" Phosa heard the sound of his spit gargling in his mouth as he chuckled.

"Phena?!"

"Run, Phosa! GO!" Phena was directly in front of her, running as fast as she could toward the metal gates that she'd only seen minutes ago. *Oh God! I hate this city!* Phosa ran as fast as she could. Thankfully, the men were slowed down by their drunken states and, after passing only a few shops, abandoned their prey.

Now completely out of breath, Phosa launched herself towards the gate and swung around to the other side, where Phena was already waiting for her. They were now in a stone courtyard, its ceiling exposing the open sky above. The space was adorned with an array of plants, both imported and indigenous, arranged in clay pots, and an ancient water fountain showing the god of fortune, Mercury, spouting water from his mouth. They both took a second to sit by the fountain just to catch their breath. After facing so many ruffians, she was grateful for the solace of the courtyard. They were easily provided for by their father's friend, the owner of the apartment block, Gaius Festus Fiernes, who supplied them with a small apartment on the second floor. He took pride in creating a beautiful garden for his renters, fresh water through the private fountain, and was even lenient when it came to rent payments.

But, even though her needs were met here, Phosa desperately wanted a home of her own. Most of the girls that she'd known as a child were married, and some even had children. Deep down, she yearned to be free of her sister's control, to have a husband of her own and a household to manage. But that hope was a far-off daydream, as their father had died unexpectedly, leaving them both with no prospects.

Phosa stood still for a moment, thinking about the years that she had spent in this courtyard, playing games with her doting father.

"Phosa! Are you coming?" Phena yelled from the middle of the staircase.

"No, I'm going to take some time here beside the fountain for a while."

"OK, take your time. But I will need help with our meal."

"Yes, ok. I'll come in a minute."

Phosa turned her attention back to the fountain, admiring the beautiful blue tinge of the water. She sat there for a few moments, enjoying the persistent hum of the city outside their gate and the peaceful silence inside. Suddenly, a rustle in the bushes nearby caught Phosa's attention. She turned her head to see a small brown rabbit cautiously hopping out into the open courtyard. Its fluffy tail twitched as it sniffed the air, seemingly unaware of Phosa's presence. A smile tugged at the corners of Phosa's lips as she watched the rabbit explore its surroundings. It was a rare moment of tranquility amidst the chaos of Rome. She wished she could be like that rabbit—free, unburdened by worries and fears.

Just then, a gentle voice interrupted her thoughts. "Enjoying some peace and quiet, are we?" Phosa turned to see Rusticus standing at a respectful distance, a kind smile on his weathered face. His eyes held a warmth that always made her feel safe and cared for.

"Yes, just taking a moment for myself."

"Yes, I imagine you'll need it. Your sister is in quite a state upstairs."

"Yes. She gets herself into many states, doesn't she?" Their shared laughter filled the courtyard and filled her heart with peace.

"She said you had quite the walk back from the parade."

"Oh, what did she tell you?" Phosa asked, worried about what Rusticus would think of her if he knew she had almost got them killed. Twice.

"Not much, just that you were stopped a few times."

"Oh, yeah. The man at the tavern was definitely the worst of them."

"Drucius again?" Rusticus asked, with obvious worry in his eyes.

"Probably. I don't know their names. Just a ruffian." Rusticus's laugh spread to Phosa despite the trauma of the memory.

"You know, I don't think I ever said thank you, Rusticus."

"Thank you for what, my lady?"

"For sticking by us, even after..." She couldn't bring herself to say the words. The loss of her mother, but mostly her father, was still too much for her.

"You and your sister are my family. I will never leave you."

Phosa forced a small, strained smile, knowing deep down that his words were likely false. It was a bittersweet realization, like the last taste of honey before the sting of a bee or the last glimmer of sunlight before the darkness of night envelops the world. Despite Rusticus's comforting words, Phosa knew that any of those encounters could have resulted in her arrest. And in that event, neither Rusticus nor Phena could have saved her.

chapter two
NERO'S RAID

Phosa trailed behind Rusticus as they climbed the stairs to their apartment. The hallway, exposed to the open air, was getting darker as daylight faded into the night. They turned left towards the door to apartment II-A and found that her neighbor had thoughtfully already lit the hallway light for them.

Thank you, Lucina! She smiled, thinking about the elderly widow who had always lived right next to her family.

"You and your sister having a meeting tonight?" An unexpected male voice asked from further down the hallway. She recognized the slight scratch in his voice. It was the gardener, Felix.

"A meeting?" Phena turned to face him, trying to sound innocent. Phosa thought she just sounded dumb.

"Yeah, a meeting, like on Jovis." *He knows when we meet?*

"Oh, those aren't meetings! They're just get-togethers with friends."

"Well, can I come, then?"

Phosa looked to Rusticus for an answer but found none. Neither of them knew what to say.

"Uh, well, sure. I guess. It's usually just a bunch of women! And we're not meeting tonight. It's tomorrow night."

"Even better!" The gardener chuckled to himself, grabbed his shovel, and turned to go down the stairs to the courtyard.

Their apartment was on the left side of the building, which overlooked the back alley just off of the Clivus Suburanus. If they had just 100 more *denari* per month, they could afford the apartment that overlooked the gardens. Phosa turned the brass key in the keyhole and opened the door. They quickly stepped into their *medianum*, which had been freshly painted a rusty red and as furnished with their parents' ancient sofa. The air inside the apartment was musty and slightly damp, with a faint scent of fresh paint lingering from the recently completed touch-up job. The familiar smell of their parent's home filled Phosa's nostrils, a mix of spices wood, and memories.

"We're here!" Phosa called to her sister, not seeing her in the medianum.

"Finally!" Her sister called from the small kitchen walled into the left side of the apartment. "I've been cooking up a storm! What took you so long?" Not wanting to get into things right away, Phosa paused to take her sandals off and wash her feet with the bowl of fresh water they kept by the door. Rusticus did the same. She then crossed the *medianum* and opened the sliding door to her small chamber.

Phosa's small chamber was sparsely furnished with just a simple bed and a small wooden desk, with a small square window and painted green shutters. The walls were a faded cream color and the sliding door was made of lightweight wood. Phosa fell onto her bed, completely exhausted from the emotion of the day.

"Phosa! Are you listening to me?" Her sister called to her from her kitchen workspace. Usually, Rusticus would make the meal.

"Yes, just give me a moment." Phosa closed her eyes, with quiet resolve to ignore her anxiety driven sister for just a few minutes. Minimally refreshed, she got up.

"We were stopped by the gardener, right Rusticus?" She asked her beloved friend and servant, who had taken to relaxing on the couch. Phosa decided to join him.

"Yes, Mistress and he wanted to know if he could come to one of your gatherings."

Phena immediately came out of the small kitchen in the corner of their apartment and into the living room; her hair in disarray, and her once clean yellow linen dress assaulted by splatters of food and oil.

"He asked you in public?"

"In the hallway."

"So, are we inviting people off the street now?"

"Well, I think that's kinda the point, isn't it?" Phosa asked, trying to sound smart.

"Well, that's true; well done, Phosa. Yes, he should come. Everyone needs to know about Jesus!"

"I mean, to tell you the truth, sister, I think it's a little scary."

"Phosa! You need to be ok with this!"

"Well, Yes, I get it. But, shouldn't we just focus on our current gathering and then..."

"You're the one that invited him..."

Then, there was a quiet but persistent knock at the door. Phosa strained her ears, unsure if she had imagined it or not. Knock! Knock! The sound came again, more insistent this time. Feeling uneasy after her encounter with the centurion and then the gardener, she was hesitant to allow anyone, friend or foe, into her tiny sanctuary.

"Phosa, are you getting that?" She yelled from the latrine. Phosa took a deep breath and got up from her relaxed position on the couch.

"Who is it?" Phosa spoke cautiously into the door.

"It's Tychicus. Open up! I'm starving, and I've got to use the latrine!" *Oh, Tychicus! I haven't seen him for over a year!* She remembered the kind and handsome face of the wandering Greek from Ephesus, who was the official mail carrier of their spiritual father, Paul.

"Phosa, let him in!"

She grabbed the doorknob and twisted it. Tychicus was a tall and lean man with dark curly hair and a well-trimmed beard. As he hurried inside, his hazel eyes darted back and forth, checking for any signs of danger. He didn't say a word until he had shut the linen curtains and slumped onto the couch.

"Hello, ladies! Forgive me; it's been a long journey, and my feet feel as if they might fall off."

They stink like they might fall off, too, Tryphosa thought, politely offering the bowl of fresh water for her guest to wash in.

"You know," Tryphena started, "as much as we love visitors, you probably shouldn't be here, seeing as how we are two single women…"
"Yes! Yes! My apologies, but I promise I have a good reason for my intrusion."

"Intrusion, well, you're not quite intruding…" Phosa answered awkwardly and with a shade of red on her cheeks.

Tychicus didn't seem to notice. "Paul has sent you his greetings." Phosa and Phena both rushed at him, excitedly as if Tychicus would read the letter to them there and then. Phosa noticed that their trusted non-Christian friend excused himself and went into one of the bedrooms for solitude. *OH, how I wish he would see the light.* Phosa returned her attention to Tychicus, her face lighting up again at the idea of receiving a personal letter from Paul. Even though neither sister had actually met him in person, Phosa felt honored by the gesture of a personalized greeting.

"Now, ladies, I don't have the time to read the letter here and now. Tryphosa, you can read, can you not?"

"Yes, sir, Yes I can." Phosa saw the glare of annoyance her sister shot her.

 "I beg you to give us a brief overview, brother," Phena said, not willing to wait for her sister to read it.

"All right, Paul sends words of encouragement and praise for the hard work that you two ladies do here in the city of Rome."

"*Mirum est!*" Phosa shouted with excitement. "Paul knows about our small house church! I wouldn't expect such a thing."

Phena smiled knowingly as if she was not surprised at all. "Please relay to Paul our most sincere and humble thanks for this personal greeting.

It is nice to be recognized, especially by someone like Paul." *There she goes again, always a ready response.* "Paul depends on people like you to share the gospel and encourage the church here in Rome since he's not been able to come himself."

"Well, you know that Peter is on his way to the city-"

"What? No, we didn't know that! Junia didn't mention his visit!"

"Oh, my apologies for making that assumption. But you really need to work hard to encourage open communication within the churches here. Do you at least have contacts within the palace and senate? As house church leaders you need to know how things are changing for our brothers and sisters. And things are changing quickly!" Phosa noticed Tychicus' face contorted from a relaxed and friendly smile to a tense and worried expression. His previously animated and lively gestures were now replaced with rigid and fidgety movements.

Phena answered for them both, "Actually, no. We are quite isolated here in the Subura, as you can imagine."

"Well, perhaps even on the streets, you've heard people talking about the mad emperor?"

"Oh, on the contrary, all I've heard lately is that he tried to abolish the taxes for everyone in the empire."

Tychicus laughed out loud at that, "Yes, yes, that is true. And actually, he was successful in the province of Greece, but that is for another conversation, surely." A smile crept onto Phosa's face as she realized she had something valuable to contribute to the conversation. She recalled a grim yet intriguing piece of information she had overheard in the market stall just the other day.

"I have heard from our contacts in the senate that Nero murdered his own mother."

"The lady Agrippina?" Phena asked, her eyes wide with surprise.

"Yes, the very one." Phosa returned.

"Wasn't she a curse upon the earth?" Phena asked rhetorically.

"Well, yes," Tychicus interjected. "But no mother deserves to be murdered."

Except for that one. They may be isolated from court drama, but they still knew about the deceitful and malicious deeds attributed to Agrippina.

"Regardless, you ladies need to understand who lives on your doorsteps and fear him. Nero is no joke. He is a curse upon the body of Christ. But one who will be defeated in the end."

"Amen!" Phena shouted in agreement.

"Hail Caesar!" Rusticus called back from the bedroom, to which Tychicus chuckled. However, the sisters remained unamused.

"Pray, what was I talking about before our most despicable emperor?

"Peter and Paul, I believe?"

"Oh, yes, I'm sure he will make his rounds, and you will be seeing him shortly. I will be visiting with Peter this coming Lunae. He is staying in a town southwest of Rome. And then I'll be reuniting with Paul before he goes to Hispania."

"Hispania?" Phena asked curiously.

"Yes, Paul has been waiting to go himself but..."

"Tychicus, excuse me," Phena interjected.

"Yes, sister?"

"Did you not say you needed the *latrina?*"

"Oh yes! Excuse me for a moment." With urgency, he bolted for the small latrine just off of the *medianium*. Once Tychicus was out of view, Phena began to pace back and forth across their *medianium*. Phosa knew her sister was up to something, sending him away.

"Sister. Did you hear that?"

"I've heard many things-"

"Peter is coming to Rome! We've been counting on Peter to come and see us and give us direction, support, protection..."

"Yes-so?"

"We must write to Junia to ensure that Peter makes a stop at our gathering. Our brothers and sisters need his encouragement. I have this bad feeling that Nero is about to bring on further troubles for us." Phena stopped pacing and looked out the window.

"Yes, but who wins in the end? Surely our Lord and Saviour does!"

"You are right, sister. Nonetheless, we must be better connected with our brothers and sisters in the city. We should draft a letter to them."

Then Phosa watched as her sister wheeled around and faced her again, this time with orders. "Get some parchment and a stylus!"

Phosa did as her sister asked and took some paper and a stylus to her from the desk in the corner of their *medianium.*

"What do you want it to say?" Phosa asked, ready to start writing.

"We need to talk."

"Ok, what else?"

"Short and sweet."

"You ladies talking about me again? Tychicus asked in jest as he came out of the *latrina.*

"No, my sister has asked me to write a letter for her. But I think that her words are too short and to the point."

Tychicus leaned over Phosa's desk and read the words, his nodding head signaling he agreed with her. "Phosa, I think you should give it more context. For instance, you could say, We would like to create a deeper connection with your church and grow in our faith with you as our mentors."

"Oh, very nice, Tychicus!" Phosa praised one writer over another.

"I suppose it does help to give more information sometimes." Phena conceded as Tychicus took the fully written sheet of paper from the desk and curled it into a roll.

"Do you have a seal?"

"No! No, we are too poor for that."

"Ok, well ladies, I must be going. Lock your doors, and always be on the alert.

"I've heard that Nero has a new legion that is stationed here in Rome and has the sole mission of arresting our brothers and sisters in Christ and carrying them off to the arena." Phosa's entire body tensed at the mention of such a force. She was aware of the challenges of being a Christian in her city, but now they seemed insurmountable. Trying to hide her fear, she turned away, but she was sure it was still written all over her face. Her sister showed no such weakness.

"Thank you for warning us, Tychicus. We will remain vigilant in the face of all dangers!" Phena responded with her usual grace and determination as if nothing in the world could intimidate her. Tychicus said his final goodbyes and then was gone.

"Did you just hear that? There's a force that has the sole purpose of killing us!" Phosa suddenly felt dizzy and was sure she would faint. Her sister must have realized this and gently set her down on the couch.

"Phosa, I know this is scary, but we are not alone. We must be determined to stand firm in our faith. And we must prepare for the worst." Her sister's words did not comfort her, as she imagined a mob of soldiers invading their apartment complex and taking all of their brothers and sisters away in chains. No trial. No chance. Just death.

"Tryphena, we're hosting brother and sisters tomorrow night. Doesn't that concern you? What if they find us? Do they know where we are?" "I guess we'll find out soon enough, but for now, get some rest. You'll need it for tomorrow." *Rest? Rest? How am I supposed to rest?*

"What, is there another festival that we have to go to?"

"No, it's a market day." Phosa let out a prolonged growl at the mention of the market. Markets were full days of physical labor in the hot sun spent with nagging and smelly customers who often loved to brag about their wealth.

And above all, markets brought in non-believers. Just one word of suspicion from a Roman meant Nero's new squad would be on her. Each day was like walking into a den of lions, and Phosa was completely uncertain of who, if any, would come out unscathed.

"Goodnight, sister. Goodnight, Rusticus!" Phena shouted as she blew out all of the oil lamps in the room and went to her room.

With shaky legs, Phosa pushed herself up and walked to her room, carefully passing by Rusticus, who was snoring on the couch. Despite her exhaustion from a day filled with intense emotions, sleep eluded her. She lay in bed, listening to the constant noise of the carts rolling past their insulae, one after another. She imagined those carts being full of rough men carrying goods into the city for the market day tomorrow. Rough men. *Men who would not hesitate to come for us if they knew about our meetings. Any of them could bring the knock of Nero's men.* Phosa wondered how her sister could just go to sleep after a well-informed brother warned them of such danger. And she just leaves me in the darkness to think and think and think. After what seemed like hours of lying awake, her mind raced with thoughts of potential disasters. Phosa's eyes finally closed, and when they did, she saw her accuser's face staring back at her. Nero. And he said, "I'm coming for you."

chapter three
LOST & FOUND

"Wake up, Phosa! We have a lot to do today!" "Ugh," Phosa moaned as she slowly peeled her eyes open; the blinding sunlight flooded in, causing her to squint and shield her face.

The distant sounds of carts and traders preparing for market day drifted in through the open window, mixing with the soft snores of Rusticus, still sleeping on the couch. Still lying in her bed, she watched her sister race away to the kitchen and just as quickly come back with a tray of breakfast and wine. The only thing that could tempt her to get out of bed in the morning was the alluring scent of her sister's honey and cheese curd oatmeal.

"Thank you, sister," Phosa said as she sipped her cold, watered-down wine and eyed up the bowl in front of her.

"We don't have much time, you know. Gaius' delivery will be here in a few minutes. I just heard the sound of Festus' donkey..."

"So Gaius' cart is not far behind..." Phosa knew the arrangement they had with Gaius just as well as her micro-manager sister.

Upon his deathbed, their father had purchased a partnership between Gaius, their distant relative, and his future son-in-law. But since their father had died before securing a match for either of his daughters, the potential for a partnership had been ignored. Now, they were relegated to being servants. Phosa ate every morsel of her oatmeal, careful not to get any on her only tunic. She stood up quickly, too quickly! Then, she walked through their sitting area, passing Rusticus' sleeping form on the couch, and over to the door where her sister had already placed a fresh basin of water for washing.

She gazed at her exhausted face in the mirror, then draped a bright red shawl over her head. The shawl always reminded her of her father and how it was the last thing he had given her before he passed away. The rough fabric mixed dyed to give off the feel of wealth, reminded her of their current powerless situation. Neither rich nor destitute, neither free nor enslaved. There was nothing to really complain about, but yet so much. When it came down to it, her father failed her by not finding a suitable husband for her. She should have had a secure situation for herself years ago. But she also knew it wasn't entirely her father's fault. Their uncle Gaius had taken all of the family's fortune when he inherited their villa in Rome and farming estate twenty miles away. Their father, who was the younger brother, had controlled the distribution of their product in the city before his passing. However, the vast expulsion of most of their clients from the city of Rome and then instability caused by Claudius' death had all but depleted their father's personal wealth. As a result, Phosa, her sister, and their one remaining servant had to live in a cramped four-room apartment instead of a spacious villa with its own garden and an abundance of servants. She tried not to think of these things as she let her day tunic slide onto her body and laced up her dirt-encrusted sandals. She did not want to carry bitterness and resentment in her heart. Junia had always taught her that Jesus wanted them to forgive everyone. *Ah, Junia.* Phosa smiled, thinking of her parents' dear friend and mentor, her deep laugh, and smiling brown eyes.

From a young age, she'd always looked up to her, for silly reasons really: the smell of her beautiful hair, the exquisite dresses she wore, and the general sense of calm that she seemed to have etched on her face. It was Junia that had led her father and mother to the new religion. Phosa could still remember the day that her father was convinced and had turned away from his precious gods. Looking back, she never would have guessed that he family would convert to this new detestable superstition, as it was called.

Not hearing any orders from her sister, Phosa decided to take it easy for a few minutes and lay back down on her bed. A few minutes of relaxation won't hurt anyone. She reached for the scroll that Tychicus had left them and unwrapped it, revealing the words that Paul himself had written for the followers in her city. Phosa was again overwhelmed by the beauty and truth in Jesus' teachings found there and couldn't deny that the way of the Romans was faulty, dark, and corrupted. She didn't want to live like them anymore. But she still didn't feel the courage and bravery that she saw in Junia, who seemed to have no fear of being caught. Every day, she prayed for more courage. She knew that without it, she'd be consumed. The emperor was known to be mad and had an unexplainable vendetta against the new superstition. "Phosa!"

"What? I mean, yes?"

"You've been standing there staring at yourself for like ten minutes!"
"I've got a lot to think about."

"Yeah, we all do. Can you do your thinking downstairs at the stall?"

Suddenly, Rusticus' lengthy legs appeared over the couch's edge, accompanied by a drawn-out and deep groan that caught the sisters' attention.

"Ladies? Oh, have I slept in? And Miss Phena made breakfast again? Oh my!"

"Don't worry yourself, Rusticus. You needed that sleep."

Phena's voice was soft and gentle, a noticeable contrast from her usually harsh tone towards her. Phosa felt her sister's sharp nails dig into her arm as she forcefully pulled her through the door and into the hallway. Despite the urge to cry out for help, Phosa stayed silent, aware that her sister would deny any violent behavior. They walked towards the stone staircase that offered two options: up towards the more crowded and less expensive apartments above or down towards the courtyard and the open streets. Phosa gently rubbed her arm where Phena's tight grip had left a mark. Phosa followed her sister down the stairs. As they got closer to the streets they could hear the commotion of carts rushing up and down the cobbled and narrow road of *Vicus Patricius.*

Phosa and her sister approached the spacious archway leading to the exit toward the bustling streets. She could hear animals braying and arguing with their owners as they dragged their vocational carts down the road at their owners' behest. *I can relate*, Phosa thought to herself.

Phosa trailed behind her sister as they rounded a sharp corner and entered the quiet market stall on the first floor of the insulae. Waiting to greet them was their great uncle Gaius, a tall and sturdy man with a constantly sweaty brow, a clean-shaven face, and bristly brown hair. His small eyes were the shade of sun-drenched manure, and his weathered face was marked with lines and sun spots. The only visible sign that Gaius was wealthy was his pristine white tunic fastened at the shoulder with a golden clasp that symbolized his nobility.

"You're late!" Guais said sternly.

"Sorry about that, sir," Phena quickly interjected. "We'll make sure it doesn't happen again."

"It's days like these that you must consider yourselves lucky I've converted to your previous superstition! Otherwise, I would not be so merciful!"

Suddenly, a fear she knew too well gripped Phosa. Phosa looked around to see if anyone had heard him speak of the Way. There were spies everywhere, hoping to find someone to bring back to Nero!

"All right, come on, then; unload the cart! I've got some shopping to do!" He waved them to the back of the market stall where she knew Gaius' carts were usually latched, ready to be unloaded with products and wares. Knowing exactly what to do, Phosa and Phena put on their linen overdresses that were kept under the stone counter of the market stall and got to work.

"Phosa, you know what to do. I'll get started on unloading the carts, and you..."

"Count the current inventory, I know. On it!"

"Hey, you shouldn't complain, you know. If I could count, I'd want that job over heavy labor!"

"I know! I know!" Phosa couldn't understand why her father had chosen to only educate her in reading, writing, and basic math. However, she was appreciative of the skills she had learned from him. Phosa walked over to the far wall of the shop and started inspecting the contents of each of the wicker bins, which were usually overflowing with seasonal produce from the family's farm.

"Celery, two sticks; Cucumber, five sticks; Cabbage, one head; Leeks, six sticks." Then she moved to the other side of the stall where the fresh fruits were placed. " dates, ten; figs, two, definitely need more figs!; apples: six." She surveyed the rest of the bins and found they were empty.

She placed the record sheet on the counter. Her job was done. Tempted not to help her sister right away, she remembered the words of the great teacher, Paul: do everything as until the Lord. *Ok, I guess I need to go help her now, then.*

Phosa walked towards the back of the market stall where her sister was hard at work organizing each of the crates into groups.

"OK, Phosa, that's the fruit section. Start with that one. And then I'll do the rest. Customers will be coming soon." Phosa silently did as she was told, bent over, and carried in the large wooden crate full of figs, dates, plums, cherries, apples, and pears.

The air was filled with the tantalizing scent of something sweet, causing her stomach to growl in hunger. She placed each juicy fruit into the proper basket, ensuring that only the best quality items made it to the inventory baskets. The other items were thrown into a bin that would be donated to the poor. Phosa updated the pricing board according to what was available while her sister marched in and out of the stall, carrying bins full of vegetables, herbs, and nuts. Seeing that the market was almost full, Phosa turned the wooden sign dangling from their roof so that the word aperta could be seen from the streets. Fully expecting the many passersby to take a sudden interest in their shop, Phosa hastily retreated to her safe place behind the counter. The moment Phosa made it to her station, the crowd of hungry bystander swarmed their stall, looking for their breakfast. The most popular purchase was usually a few pears. Sometimes, morning customers would also purchase their breakfast from the hot counter, which featured Phena's legendary hot oatmeal and some freshly baked bread, which Gaius offered to his customers through Janis, their third-party baker. It being just a day before the *parentalia* festivities, most people came in for a bit and then quickly left to continue with their household preparations. But two rather richly dressed Roman women broke the mold and came in to sit down at one of two tables set out for patrons. Both women were clearly of *patrician* class, one wearing a pristinely white silk tunic and what appeared to be a solid gold belt around her waist.

Her rich chestnut brown hair was gathered together in an expert bun and her ears were supporting the massive weight of yet more gold, studded with precious stones. Her companion was dressed slightly more modestly but still in fine garments made of embroidered silk and clipped together by gold brooches at her shoulders. Phosa pondered the unusual posture of these women, lounging in the small wooden chairs instead of sitting up properly.

"Slave! Wine!" Phosa couldn't stand it when women of rank assumed that anyone working a regular job was a slave. It took every ounce of her self-control not to dump the entire contents of her wine vessel onto this sour lady's beautifully crimped blond hair.

"Here you are, my lady. Do you require any refreshment, a cake or bread perhaps? Both freshly baked." The woman merely waved her hand in reply. Phosa was happy to take her place behind the counter again but much less enthusiastic about their conversation.

"How have you been, Flauvia?" The woman in the heavy gold earrings started, "Your household? The children? And what plans have you for *parentalia*?"

"My dear Claudia, you already know the answers to those questions! After all, my husband speaks to you more than he speaks to me."

"Well I'll tell you something then, You know I heard that Agrippina, may the gods watch over her, before she met her untimely demise, had been slowly converting to the strange ways of that new religion." Claudia raised her wine glass to her mouth but didn't drink. Phosa looked up from her task behind the counter, eager to listen to what the women were saying.

"What new religion? There are so many strange traditions that reach our city." Flauvia only looked half interested in the answer.

"You know, the followers of the..." Then Claudia bent over closer to Flauvia's ear to whisper. "Crucified man."

"Oh, yes. How despicable!"

"Indeed! But you know Nero would never suffer such superstitious nonsense."

"Of course not!" Flauvia's face erupted into an indignant certainty. "And no matter the will of the Emperor, their kind can never be accepted in our great city and empire. What with their cannibalistic rituals, drunken feasts, and exclusive meetings? Not to mention their inexcusable lack of hygiene!"

"Why, it's a wonder that Jupiter himself doesn't call upon all the forces of the heavens against these superstitious followers."

"I couldn't agree more." Flauvia placed her wine goblet down on the table and started to rise from her seat. Neither woman gave Phosa even a glance before leaving the establishment.

After serving breakfast to what seemed like half of Rome's inhabitants, Phosa finally sat down on the dusty floor of the shop, completely exhausted. She could hear the distant singing of the vestal virgins on Capitoline Hill, which signaled the hottest hour of the day.

"Looks like it's time for a siesta!" Phena announced, appearing from the backroom.

"Oh, praise the Lord! That was a crazy morning! Did you see all the people that came in here?!"

"Yes, you did a great job, sister. Now, have some lunch." Phena motioned for her to sit beside her at the bar stools that were supposed to be for the patrons only.

"You sure?"

"Yeah, Gaius won't ever know." Phosa reluctantly agreed with her sister and relaxed on the soft cushion of the stool.

"What do we have for lunch, Phena?" Phena didn't answer. Phosa turned around, and to her astonishment, there was no one in the shop. "Phena?" Phosa shouted for her sister from the back of the shop. Still no answer.

What could have happened to her in a few split seconds? Phosa thought of Tychicus' words last night. *Maybe those women saw my sign and reported us! I've always known it's just a matter of time.*

"Phena! Phhhenna!" Phosa's voice grew louder, filled with desperation. She hurried to the back room, hoping to find her there, but she was nowhere to be seen. Panic set in as she realized that she was gone. *What am I going to do without her?*

Suddenly, the eerily quiet street was awakened by the stir of feet pounding against the sidewalk. Someone was running towards her. Phosa's entire body stiffened, ready for whoever was coming for her. A flood of fresh air flowed through her body, her tightened muscles released seeing her sister's face. Phosa ran towards her, not caring about the puzzled stares from the passersby.

"Phena! What happened? Where did you go? I'm so mad at you right now!

"Mad, why?" Phena asked, still out of breath from her long walk in the heat.

"I thought you'd been arrested, ok? I thought someone had denounced us!" Phosa shouted; her voice was shaky and filled with panic.

"You thought, in the five seconds that I was gone, a soldier had come to take me away?"

"Yes! You scared me half to death..."

"Are you that worried about being reported?" Phosa looked down, but she couldn't see her sister's judgmental gaze. She knew that she should be more fearless and ready to suffer for Jesus, but...

"I'm terrified, Phena. Every night, I'm haunted by Nero's devilish gaze and sure that he will find me. Some nights, I can even smell the smoke of the flames as I am lit on fire for the illumination of the mad emperor's gardens."

"Phosa! Shhh! Not here!" Phena's hands were suddenly on her wrist, and her body was unwillingly dragged into the privacy of their stall. Phosa ripped her hand from her sister's rough grasp and started to pace the only aisle of their empty stall. The panic that had consumed her earlier was still lingering in her body, reluctant to subside.

"Phosa! You can't just say anything you want about Nero in the streets! He does not take kindly to being criticized by his people; everyone knows that!" Phosa could see that her sister was furious with her. And if she wasn't so upset herself, she wouldn't have blamed her.

"OK, ok. We just need to take a second to relax. OK? Sit." Phosa did as she was told.

"I can't keep pretending that I'm strong. I don't think I am!"

"It's ok, sister. We are all afraid! But listen to me..." Phena took her sister's hand in hers and lifted her chin so that she was forced to look into her eyes. "We are different than the pagans around us. We have hope of eternal life after this life is over. Remember that. One day, we might rise from the shadows and face hungry lions in the circus, as many of our brothers and sisters have before us. Or we might be lamps for Nero's gardens like you have dreamed. But, that pain will only last a few short moments, and then we will be with Jesus."

Phosa took a deep breath, and the tenseness that she'd felt all over her body faded. She fell into her sister's embrace and stayed there for a few moments.

"So, where were you?"

"I was merely visiting my Lucius and his new mare, Stella."

"Oh." That's pretty harmless. Phosa took a deep breath, relieved there was no immediate danger.

"Lucius wants to train her to be in the races. Her name is Stella. So it fits.

"I didn't take you two ladies for *circensiani!*" A mysterious male voice teased. There in the doorway of their shop was a tall young man with handsome features and curly brown hair stood in the doorway to their shop, his shockingly blue eyes gazing at them both.

Both the sisters looked up from the paper startled, still thinking about the possibility of getting found out by the authorities. But Phosa's feared faded away when she recognized his familiar face.

"Oh Stallio, it's just you!"

Phosa and her sister had met him last year at Junia's house church on Quirinal Hill. He was a highly educated accountant, though slave, owned by a senator Publius Clodius Thrasea Paetus.

"So it is the Blues or the Reds?!" Stallio waved to Phosa, who was still sitting at a table at the back of the shop.

"Oh, Stallio, neither, really. We're not as serious as all that!" The three of them laughed in unison.

"What brings to you tour shop? I mean, it's the middle of the day and you do live all the way across the city?"

"Usually, the master has me come to the market in the morning and visit some of his clients, but this morning, I was very busy transcribing some letters for him and delivering them all over the city."

"Oh, there's news then."

"Yes, but first, I need fruit."

"We have that." Stallio let out a chuckle as he started to peruse the wall of baskets full of fruit. He filled up his wooden crate with generous amounts of figs and pears, with some exotic nuts that usually were sold out by the end of the day.

"Figs, and pears?" Phosa asked, coming closer to help the handsome man with his purchase.

"Yes, the master wants the chef to try a new recipe. You can't go wrong with figs and pears!" Stallio turned to look directly at Phosa, placed a small fresh fig in his mouth, and charmingly whispered,

"So delicious!" Phosa closed her eyes and tried very hard to resist the charm that exuded from this gorgeous blond Greek slave. She knew that as a follower of Jesus, she was held to a higher standard than any pagan woman. Openly flirting with customers in her stall was never considered respectable, but even less so now. She honestly wanted to be pure of heart and be an obedient servant of Jesus, but men like Stallio made that goal very difficult.

"Phosa, are you busy later?" The question hung in the air expectantly as Phosa tried to find the right words to respond. In her mind, she wanted to scream, "Yes! Yes!" but her mouth refused to cooperate. Instead, she stuttered, "Well, I...uh..."

"Phosa? Hello? We have a meeting tonight." Phena reminded her, not specifying what type of meeting they were having in case someone else stepped into their stall.

"Uh, yes." Phosa smiled nervously. "I'll be busy."

"All right, another time then?" Stallio gently smiled and lightly touched her hand with his.

"Yes, another time. Thank you, Stallio."

"Sorry to disrupt this moment you two are clearly having, but have you found everything you need?"

"Yes, The figs and pears. Thank you, ladies. As always, you have been most helpful!"

"Thank you, Stallio. Have a lovely day!"

"Goodbye!" Phosa waved as the young man left the stall and headed down the street, which had become busy with shoppers, vendors, and religious officials.

"What are you doing?"

"What me?"

"Yes, you!"

"I didn't do anything..."

"Flirting! Openly flirting! Do you even know for sure if he is a Christian?"

"We'll. I've gotta marry someone, right? And what am I going to do, interview them before I court them?"

"Sister! You know you have to be careful! And there's the little problem of him being a slave."

"Wait for a second; some slaves are better off financially than we freed people..."

"That might be true, but your children would be slaves."

"Uhgh, Phena, you're always such a nag! I'm not marrying him or anyone else this second, so what's all this....?"

"Excuse me?" Both sisters jumped as another voice was thrown into the mix. They turned to face a sweet and shy young woman with blue eyes that bordered on purple, golden blond locks, and cheeks so rosy that she looked like she might be fevered. She made her way directly to the counter, something most customers did not do.

"Yes?" Phosa quickly gained her composure, "What can we do for you?" Phena rushed forward to greet the woman. She must have noticed the golden bangles on her arms and the pure silver interlacing that decorated her *tutulus*.

Everything from her fine jewelry, the sheen of her crimson cape, and her floral perfume indicated she was of the senatorial class.

"*Domina*, if you are looking for exotic fruits and vegetables, then you're in the right place. Your cook is sure to be thrilled by our selection. How many will be attending your feast?" Phena asked presumptuously. The young woman smiled graciously and leaned in towards the girls to whisper, "Actually, I'm looking for Tryphosa and Tryphena."

"Well, you've found us. How can we help you?"

"Junia sent me. I have a letter for you."

"How do you know Junia?"

The young woman's blue eyes flickered with something that seemed like hesitation before her face broke into a gracious smile. "Junia Maia Joventus; she is the leader of my current house church." Phosa wasn't sure what to think of this high-born woman. *She could easily be a spy. And it means nothing that she knows Junia's names. This could just be a trap!* Phosa looked at her sister, hoping to see reserved caution and was disappointed. She only saw determination and an eagerness to hear more.

MY DEAR SISTERS IN CHRIST, TRYPHOSA, AND TRYPHENA.

YOU ARE IN GRAVE DANGER. WE ALL ARE. BUT OUR CONCERN HAS TRUMPED OUR DESIRE TO BE DISCREET SO WE ARE JOINING YOU FOR YOUR MEETING THIS EVENING. I MUST COMMUNICATE TO YOU WHAT I KNOW I CANNOT IN A LETTER. BE VIGILANT IN YOUR PRAYERS. WE NEED OUR LORD MORE THAN EVER BEFORE.

YOUR FELLOW WORKER AND SISTER IN CHRIST, JUNIA.

"Ok, why don't you come with me into the back to discuss this? Phosa, you can come; just keep an eye out for customers." Phena led them to the back of the stall, where the animals were kept.

"Please excuse the smell, Domina."

"There's no need to address me formally. My name is Carius Quintus Junas. I am Junia's sister. Here is the letter." Carius pulled a fine parchment from inside her *stola*. It was sealed with the stamp of Junia's house. Carius remained silent as she watched Phena snap open the seal. She looked over the paper and then handed it to Phosa.

"Is Junia ok? And the other believers are they—"

"There were three men arrested from the group, slaves of Junia and easy targets for Nero's men. Junia has gone into hiding with her husband. But rest assured, she is securing connections with other house churches in the city for all of her flock." *Oh, thank God Junia is ok.* Phosa thought, relieved.

"So, what exactly happened?" Phena asked.

"Roman centurions came upon Junia's villa while they were hosting a house church.

"Were you there when the Romans came? Do they know your face?" "I was able to escape. I do not know if they saw my face." *Oh dear God, have mercy! Please protect us from the brash actions of this silly woman. She clearly does not know the danger she is in.*

"So you were there?"

"Yes! But I escaped."

"Did anyone see you come here?"

"Maybe, I'm not sure...I tried to be careful." A look of unease and trepidation crossed Phena's features. She scanned the room, her focus shifting between the two doorways that gave a view to the streets beyond, clearly uncertain about her own well-being.

"Look at me." Phena took hold of her face and forced her to concentrate her gaze on her. "We are all in danger because you have come here."

"Yes, I am sorry, but it is not my arrival in your stall that has put you in danger."

"What do you mean?"

"Don't be fooled! If you belong to the Way, you're in danger whether they know about you or not. Nero is diligent and vindictive, merciless. I've even heard that he has an elite network of spies that operate in the city, looking for any opportunity to wreak havoc, start riots, and even steal, murder, and commit arson. All to pin it on the Christians."

Phosa was sure that she would either faint or throw up right there in the middle of their uncle's market stall. "It's only a matter of time..." Carius continued, suddenly spurred on by the warning that had been engraved on her heart like iron.

"So what are you saying exactly?"

The young woman's expression shifted from timid naivety to one of determined wisdom and resilience. "Stealth, safety, secrecy. These are useless words to us who follow the Way. Instead of worrying about our safety, we should be thinking about spreading the good news, knowing that we could die by Nero's hand at any time. His sword stretches across the entire city of Rome, and his ferocious..."

"Yes, OK. Listen. Please do not speak like this to my sister." Phena turned to look at her sister, who was still standing behind the marble counter of the takeaway bar, probably counting out their cut of the sales for today.

"Let us get back to my original question. Your house church, where is it?"

"Yes, we have a house church on the second floor of this building. It meets tonight. Come if you can, but be cautious."

"Ok, we'll be there."

"Whose we?"

"About six followers from Junia's church."

"Six? No, you cannot bring six people; that would garner too much attention. And anyway, we already have five and a very small apartment." Carius only smiled and then turned to take her leave. "See you tonight," she yelled without turning to face them again and was gone.

"She didn't even buy anything!" Phosa complained from behind the counter.

"No, she came to give."

"Give what?"

"Fear."

chapter four
THE SECRET MEETING

The two sisters sat in silence, still shaken by the domina's visit. Phosa felt her hands grow cold as she folded up the paper and handed it back to her sister, desperate to separate herself from the danger spoken there.

"Ok, well, at least Junia is safe. And she's coming tonight."

"Yes, that's good, right?"

"Yes, that's good. It will be good to see our mentor and friend."

"What are we going to do? Churches are being raided. Brothers and sisters arrested. Paraded."

"We're going to pray and rejoice in the Lord. For He is in control."

The sisters loaded up their baskets with all of the produce that had not been sold that day and gathered Gaius' money from the sales in a pouch he'd given them for such a purpose. Phosa heaved the weighty baskets of produce onto the street while Phena secured the storefront with a heavy iron gate and locked it securely behind them.

"You extinguished the fires?" Phena asked her sister, as she was turning the key.

"Yes."

"And you have the money?"

"No I gave it to Festus."

"OK, good! And all the candles..."

"Yes, sister, the shop is fully closed up!"

"Ok, OK!"

They walked five steps to the left of the storefront, both of them carrying pots of leftover food that they didn't sell throughout the day. Within a few seconds, they were through the main archway, inside the courtyard, and ascending the staircase up to the second floor. The columned corridor was lined with chamber pots and other unmentionables that would need to be cleared before their guests arrived. Phosa looked at the state of the corridor and instinctively knew that she would be assigned to the task. The sisters walked into the apartment and simultaneously fell onto the couch, both completely exhausted from the long day at the market stall. Phosa looked around for Rusticus, who was nowhere to be seen. He usually spent most of the day in their apartment, although what he did all day in such a tiny space was anyone's guess.

"Where is Rusticus?"

"How should I know? The man does as he pleases."

Then a thought entered Phosa's mind, one that she didn't much like.

"Phena?"

"Yes?"

"Have you ever wondered if Rusticus is on our side?"

Phosa observed Phena's brow furrow with a mixture of indignation and confusion."No! What a thing to ask! He's always been loyal to our family. And anyway, what are you suggesting?"

"Nothing, I just, I mean, he overhears a lot. And he's not a follower of the Way."

"So?"

"He could be yet another spy! Aren't we supposed to be on the lookout?"

"Rusticus is not spying on us! How ridiculous! Really, sister, you need a nap or something!"

The sisters set about cleaning up their small apartment in preparation for their guests, who would be arriving in just a few hours. After taking care of the chamber pots in the hallway, washing the cement floors, dusting out the carpets in the corridor, wiping down all the surfaces, and fluffing the few pillows they had as decorations, Phosa was ready to fall down and sleep.

"Sister, come on! We can't rest yet; Rusticus isn't here, and the food needs to be prepared. Can you lend a hand?" Phosa groaned in response. All she wanted to do was sleep. She wished they could just reschedule their house church meeting for another night, but she knew that last-minute changes like that were never well-received.

Phosa used all the strength that she had left to lift herself from the couch and head into their small kitchen to look at the state of the copper pots that they had brought home from the stall. She lifted the lid of the larger one and saw that it was empty. *Sold out, great!* Then, she lifted the lid of the frying pan. *Four mackerels! That's enough to feed five thousand!* She thought with a snicker. *We just need some bread.*

"Phena, do we have any bread?"

"On the middle wall shelf," Phena answered quickly.

Phosa reached over to the middle shelf and found four loaves. *When did she have time to bake these?* "I got them from Janis." *I hate when she does that, it reads my mind. It's creepy!*

"Ok!" As usual, Phena was on the ball.

Phosa's spine tingled as she heard the distinct sound of someone tapping on the door. *Here we go.* Phena rushed from their stone sink towards the door, an excited grin on her face. Phosa was only steps behind her, and already there were four extra bodies in her small living room. She didn't recognize any of them. Maybe Carius sent them... They all greeted each other with warm smiles and friendly kisses on the cheek, exchanging pleasantries and engaging in the usual small talk that comes with a first meeting of the day.

"Come in, brothers and sisters. Quickly." Phena ushered them in, showing them the couch where they were instructed to make themselves comfortable.

"Wine, friends?"

"Why, yes, please, miss." One of their mysterious guests replied.

"Tryphena, but you can call me Phena, and your name?"

"Fortuna."

A pleasant smile graced the middle-aged woman's face as she pushed her unruly chestnut brown hair behind her. Phena observed the woman's clothing and determined that she was part of the plebeian class, much like herself. The tunic made of light brown wool and the scuffed leather sandals were clear indicators of her status.

"Please excuse me a moment. I'll be back with some wine." Phena left with a gracious smile and bounded towards the culina, where her sister Phosa was still working away.

"How's the food coming, sister?"

"Who are those people?" Phosa countered, not answering her sister's question. "I haven't fully figured that out. But I'm assuming they were sent by either Carius or Junia."

"I thought we told Carius not to send so many..."

"Well, she wanted to send six. Four is better."

"But still! And where is Carius herself? Didn't she say she was coming?"

"I have no idea. Let's just focus on who is here. Can you bring out a plate of cheese and grapes, and then later on we'll serve the fish and bread." Phena commanded, pouring wine into a goblet. Then she disappeared into the living room again.

Phena, passing the goblet to Fortuna, took a closer look at the rest of her visitors. The other woman in the group had long, curly red hair tied into a tight bun. Her skin was flawless, creamy, and smooth, giving the impression that she'd never worked a day in the sun. She was holding hands with one of the men, presumably her husband.

The man, with rugged features and weathered hands, wore a simple tunic that hinted at a life of hard work. His gaze was gentle as he looked around the modest apartment, taking in the small decorations and the warmth of the flickering oil lamps. The red-haired woman nodded appreciatively, her demeanor poised and graceful.

"Thank you for welcoming us into your home. My name is Livia, and this is my husband, Gaius."

"Livia, Gaius, my sister, and I welcome you to our humble home. Our servant Rusticus is currently out." *God knows where.* Phosa whispered to herself from the *culina.*

"Otherwise, he would be here to welcome you as well."

"And you are all followers, I presume?"

"My sister and I have been followers of the Way for a few years and were converted by our gracious and loving father, who has recently departed."

"My condolences, and now it seems you live out your days alone. Did he not arrange a marriage for the two of you before leaving you? And are you not dowered?"

"Livia!" Her husband scolded her. "It isn't your place. I apologize for my wife."

"No, that is not necessary. She is correct in her assumptions. Our father did not leave us with any marriage arrangements. But we have an agreement with our uncle which provides for our upkeep."

"That's perfectly respectable." Gaius returned politely.

"And you are coming to us from Junia, are you not?" This time, Fortuna spoke up, "Yes, it seems you have heard the news then."

"Yes, but let's wait for Junia to arrive and tell us more." *Good call, sister. These walls are quite flimsy.* Phosa thought to herself, overhearing the whole conversation. The fourth member of this mysterious band of followers was an elderly man who had remained completely silent since his arrival and, indeed, had barely moved since sitting down on the couch. Phosa observed that his unruly tendrils of hair, a mix of grey and brown, seemed to be intentionally styled with olive oil in that precise area. *Maybe he hasn't been very lively because he doesn't want to disturb the intricacies of his hair.* Phosa wondered to herself, thinking about how uncomfortable he looked. He wore a simple yellow tunic to his knees with a broad brown leather belt around his waist. Around his neck was a wooden carving of an anchor, which was either a Christian sign or a souvenir from the docks. *A middle-class Roman, I would imagine. Maybe a merchant?*

"And, may I ask your name, *domine?*"

"Rufus Loxus Stepahanus, at your service!" He recited as if reading from a book.

"Tryphena Neverna Festus, at yours."

"Oh, bringing out the long names, are we?" her sister teased from the culina. The group on the couch laughed, and the mood was lightened. The mood was lightened even more when Phosa suddenly emerged from the kitchen with a tray of cheese and grapes, which she placed on the table in front of the guests and then invited them to eat. She noticed that one of the guests was no longer sitting on the couches but walking around the room, gazing at some of their decorations scattered around the room. Phosa stood behind the blond woman, whom she remembered was named Fortuna.

"Excuse me, Fortuna, is it?" Phosa asked gently.

"Yes, that's right. Please excuse me; I was just looking at this idol. A relic from the past is it?" Phosa felt a slight blush creep onto her cheeks as she realized they still had some remnants of their pagan beliefs on display. "I'm embarrassed to say it is."

"Minerva?"

"Yes. Minerva. Before he converted, my father had a particular attachment to Minerva. He valued wisdom, justice, and victory."

Fortuna hesitantly returned the idol to its original spot; her face turned downward awkwardly. Phosa intervened, grabbing the idol from the shelf, fully intent on throwing it out the window when she had the chance. Phosa's sister's eyes bore into her with an intense, fiery glare, her eyebrows drawn together in disapproval. She knew exactly what that stare meant. *We'll talk about that later.*

"Can I have your attention, ladies and gentlemen?" Phena shouted from the middle of the living room. "We hope you've enjoyed the food and drink. There will be some more as the night progresses. I know that I've made your acquaintance, but for those of you who haven't met my sister yet, may I introduce Tryphosa or Phosa if you like." Phosa lowered her head slightly as all attention shifted to her. The visitors smiled, nodded their heads, and offered varied gestures and 'hellos' in return. Then, a gentle knock grazed, followed by the creaking of the door as Phena opened it. Three familiar faces emerged.

"Uh, Phena! Nice to see you!" Felinas greeted her warmly as the other two guests shuffled in.

"Hurry, come inside!" she urged, quickly ushering the guests into the room.

After closing the door behind them, she turned and wrapped her arms around all three of them in a warm hug. These were the familiar faces of loyal supporters who frequently joined them in their own home.

"Linus! It's great to see you! And you, Cressita! We missed you last week. And how have you been, Julia? Welcome! Welcome! Please sit! The couch is full, but there is space on the floor." Phena gestured towards the pillows that Phosa was arranging along the far wall.

"We are being joined by some of Junia's house church followers this evening. We were just getting started when you..."
TAP! TAP! TAP!

"That's the door again," Phosa stated the obvious. Phena headed back towards the door, and opened it slowly. Before her stood two of her most treasured friends and mentors, Junia and Festus.

"Oh, Junia!" Phena stretched out her arms to greet her friend. Junia stood tall with a warm, welcoming smile. Her long, gray hair was pulled back in a neat braid, and her face was lined with wisdom, with no indication of her recent hardships. Festus, beside her, was shorter and regale-looking with his pure white Pella and crimson red shawl; the warm light of the room reflected off of his bald head. Festus shuffled past the couch and took a seat with the others on the floor, evidently very comfortable and familiar with his friend's apartment.
The once quiet room was now filled with exuberant chatter and laughter as everyone greeted each other joyfully. Phosa took a second to look out the window at the streets below. The lamplighters were already outside about their work. The blazing heat of the day was fading, making way for a cool moon to take its place. Preparing for the inevitable danger that would soon come their way, she tightly shut the wooden shutters on every window in their apartment before returning to greet her guests.

"Ladies and Gentlemen, can I have your attention again?" The group's raucous laughter slowly died down to a murmur, and all eyes turned to Phena.

"Yes, thank you! It seems like everyone is here now, so we are going to start. I'd like to first welcome Junia and her husband Festus." Junia smiled at the group and said, "Thank you for having us. If I may, I'd like to make an announcement."

"Please..." Phena responded.

"I know some of you may have already heard our news, but I wish to ensure that you have all received the proper warning. Our people are in danger. While we have never been accepted by the state or people of Rome, we have never before been considered the enemy as we are now. Just last night, my house on Quirinal Hill was sacked by the *cohortes urbane*, Nero's gang of vipers."

"Now, my dear, you must be more careful with your words."

"My dear husband, I must speak the truth. These deceitful individuals entered our household without invitation, looted our possessions, violated my servant girls, and took into custody some of my most trusted companions." Junia's voice wavered slightly as she struggled to speak, her breaths coming out in short gasps as she tried to keep her composure. There was a hint of anger in her tone, underlying the fear and sadness that threatened to overwhelm her.

"Just today, we learned from our friend, whom we shall not name here for his safety, that the men who sacked my home are members of the newly commissioned elite squad of spies called the *frumentarii*."

Phosa felt a heavy weight descend upon her chest, an impending sense of doom that she couldn't shake off. She exchanged a quick, worried glance with Tryphena,

whose usually calm demeanor was now etched with concern. Junia continued, her voice steady despite the turmoil within her.

"I do not tell you these things to sew fear into your hearts. But I must urge all of you to be vigilant, to watch your steps and guard your words. The darkness that looms over us is relentless. Our faith will be tested, but we must stand firm in our beliefs." Festus, sitting beside his wife, placed a reassuring hand on her shoulder as a gesture of solidarity. "And we must remember that even as the darkness is threatening the light, we must love those who are blinded in the dark. Above all, we must show the unbelievers in our lives the love of Christ and the difference that He makes in us."

"Excuse me, domina. We already are so different!" Chimed in Jason Jovestus, the doctor-slave of renowned lawyer Felix Julius Longius, a long-time attendee of their home church, who must have just slipped into their meeting unnoticed.

"In my master's household, I am a constant source of trouble because I refuse to sleep with my master. Every time I reject his advances, I get punished with floggings. The other slaves in the house pity me and do not understand why I won't just give in to the master's demands. And from the Roman perspective, my master does nothing wrong expecting this detestable thing from his slave."

The group was silenced by the harsh reminder of Rome's unforgiving laws, their expressions a mix of shock to anger to sadness. Some looked down at the ground, others had tears in their eyes, and a few clenched their fists in frustration. Phosa could only feel pity as she gazed into the sorrowful eyes of the helpless slave among them; she was overwhelmed with guilt every time she complained about her own life. In hindsight, her complaints seemed trivial in comparison to the hardships and lack of freedom this slave endured.

Junia finally broke the silence. "Jason, is it?"

"Yes, domina."

"Jason, you have endured much for the Lord. While you may not reap any reward here or your obedience to Christ, you will surely be rewarded one day when we are all reunited with Him in glory."

The words that Junia spoke lingered in the air, bringing a sense of peace and hope to the previously sorrowful faces within the group. Phosa looked around, wondering if anyone had ever heard another follower speak like that. The thought of receiving treasures in heaven captivated her, and she hoped it was true.

"Thank you, domina. No one has ever given me such encouragement. I am truly grateful."

Then Linus spoke up. "I agree that we are already so different than the unbelievers. Just yesterday I bumped into a fellow brother in the market, and as we were leaving we embraced. I suppose because this friend of mine was a slave, the Roman guard watching us immediately pulled the man from me and threw him across the street, almost into oncoming traffic. It was a horrible sight. And all for an embrace! We are different. We don't have to brandish ourselves with one of those fish behind our ears or on our shoulders. Rome knows."

"Yes," Jason agreed, his eyes alight with fear and rage. "and it's only a matter of time before we are led away in chains just like..."

"Sisters! Brothers!" Junia stood up and spoke to the whole group, "Remember, our current afflictions are nothing when we think of our coming eternal home in Heaven with Jesus. Our earthly battles do not matter. What matters is that we finish the race well, as Paul would say. Our main goal is not to disappear into the Roman masses and go undetected. Our goal is to stand out in exactly the way you are saying and share Jesus' love with the Romans.

So, instead of being in perpetual fear of being found out and led away to the lions, as you've seen happen to many brothers and sisters, rejoice! Pray that you may join them and go to eternity with Christ all the sooner."

Phosa couldn't tell if it was her head spinning or her whole body. Her vision blurred, and she was sure her meager supper would soon make a reappearance on the lap of one of her guests. She could barely make out their faces, but she was certain they were looking at her with disdain and questioning her ability to host such a gathering.

Am I even good enough to be counted amongst these warriors for Christ? All she could think of was the agonizing fear that took hold of her body, just thinking of the man she had seen only a few days ago as he was led out to his death. And the sheer terror in his eyes.

"Yes," Phena signaled her approval of her guest's message, "Junia is right. We should all welcome the fate of a martyr, as that would bring glory to our precious Saviour, Jesus Christ, who gave up everything for us. But until that day comes, we are placed here in Rome for one purpose: to show the love of Christ to the Romans and to preach the good news."

"How can we preach?" Fortuna asked, who had come with the four followers from Junia's house. "We are just women. We are under the care of our fathers, sons, and husbands. We do not speak for ourselves."

Phena looked over at Junia to signal that she should answer the question. "Well, Fortuna, you're right. It is commonplace for a woman to be under the protection of a man, and very few of us have the chance to live our lives in complete freedom. We are told, for good reason, to chaperone and would likely be flogged if we preached in the forum. But what you can do is tell the people that you do life with that Jesus loves them and saves them from their sins and the darkness of this world."

Fortuna nodded her head and submissively turned her head towards the woven carpet on the floor. "OK, let's have a break for a few minutes." Phena interjected". "Be sure to eat some fish and some bread, which we'll bring out from the *culina* shortly. You can use the latrine just inside the second door on the left. And please let me know if you'd like some more wine."

The scent of fresh bread and fish wafted through the air, making Phosa's stomach growl with hunger. The smell of wine also lingered, tempting her to take a sip. Her sister's gentle voice could be heard in the background, instructing the group and offering them refreshments. She was thankful for her sister's natural ability to entertain and host guests, as she knew she did not possess the same talent. Her sister's abilities were like a shining beacon, admired and appreciated by all. Meanwhile, she was still uncertain of her own talents and how to harness them. Lost in her own thoughts, Phosa went to the *culina* to dispose of her goblet and grab herself some food when her sister gently grabbed her by the arm.

"Are you ok?"

"Yes, yes. I'm fine. I'm just..."

"What? Do you need a few minutes alone? That would be ok if you did. You could always take some air in the courtyard. But please don't go out onto the streets. They're not safe at this hour."

"Phena! I'm not going anywhere. I'm just hungry." Phena nodded and then returned to their guests. "Alright, everyone, the break is over." Her words were like a signal flare bursting in the air, calling the scattered group back to order and reminding them of the fleeting night. All returned to their spots in the living room when Linus held up his hand. "Yes, Linus, would you like to speak?"

"Yes, I'd like to ask Junia and her husband a question."

"Go on then."

"How did you manage to escape the raid of the *frumentarii*? As the *paterfamilias*, wouldn't you be responsible under Roman law?"

"We are only standing here before you because my husband is a magistrate and understands our rights under Roman Law."

"Which are few and far between for sure."

"Yes," Festus chimed in, "but they were enough to help us in this instance. Despite their brutality, the guards were very reasonable when I brought up the rights of a Roman citizen, that they required a warrant signed by a magistrate, and that Roman citizens had the right to remain in their home until such a time as their trial."

"Yes, he was brilliant! The officers did not have a warrant, so we asked them with all due respect and reverence to please leave our home until they do have a warrant."

"So, you didn't deny that you were followers of the Way?" Phosa asked bravely.

"No, and we would never do such a thing."

"Of course not," Phosa replied in an attempt to save her dignity. "So you can no longer operate your house church out of your house then?"

"No, we have to move to another venue. We have rented a warehouse on the far west end of town. Those areas are rarely monitored, and no neighbors are watching our door."

"Praise the Lord! His work continues forever, Amen!"

"Amen!"

"Hey, uh, while we are still on the subject of the Romans, has anyone here been accused of being an atheist?" Linus asked a glint of mischief in his eyes. A few guests shook their heads or said No, but then Cressida said, "Yes, I've heard that one!"

"Is it not odd? They also seem to dream up all of these diabolical rituals that we do together."

Their faces contorted like a field of freshly turned soil, the creases around their eyes digging deep with shock and disapproval as they processed Cressida's words.

"Such as?"

"Drunkenness, orgies, and incestual relations. Gluttonous feasts."

"Hypocrites, the lot of them!"

"Here! Here!"

"Wait, why would they think we are perverted incestuous drunks?"

"We call one another brother and sister, and some exchange kisses of peace." Phosa could sense the unease among the guests lounging on the couches as they considered what this statement might mean for them. Being linked to wild parties and unrestrained behavior was the exact opposite of their desired image.

"So what are we going to do? About the raids, I mean."

"Nothing. Let them make their accusations. And all the while, we will show them the love of Christ."

"How?"

"Junia has commissioned some artwork and jewelry to be fashioned for our neighbors."

"Yes, and I think I'll have my cook produce some honey cakes daily for a while, and Julianus can deliver them to each of our neighbors."

"That's a good idea."

"Finally, friends, If you remember anything from this night, let it be this," Junia paused, looking like she was choosing her words carefully. The guests leaned in, hanging on every word, their hearts pounding with anticipation of what was to come next. In that moment, her words felt like a shield, protecting them from the storm of persecution raging outside the walls of their gathering.

Then she began again, a steely determination on her face, "We will face persecutions and dangers all day long as Christians. We should be expecting it. But, we do not disobey the law of Christ in the pursuit of defending ourselves. We should lie down and let them take us to our eternal seat with Christ. Do not trouble yourselves with what your fate might be. The Lord has already ordained your end, and that will not change no matter how much you worry. Instead, worry about the pagans all around us who do not know the Truth."

Phosa's heart raced in her chest as she listened to the confident woman, the one who had introduced her to Christianity, boldly delivering a message of courage to a room full of scared and confused individuals. Guilt flooded her heart as she desperately wished for the meeting to end. She couldn't bear to hear any more words of despair and hardship.

"We follow Jesus's teachings and turn the other cheek," Junia said, tilting her head to show her smooth, unmarked cheeks.

"Yes! That's right."

The rest of the group enthusiastically nodded their heads in agreement with Junia's delegation, their faces full of hope.

Fearful thoughts raced around and around in Phosa's mind, and accidentally, one escaped, "What happens if we are threatened and become homeless? Dispersed with no friends?" As soon as the foolish question left her mouth, she wished she could take it back. Junia simply smiled, her gentle voice wrapping around me like a warm hug. "Pray. God is faithful to protect you and provide for you,"

"I think Phosa is wondering if there is a safe house set up by the community of Christ here in Rome." Phena piped in, seeking to find the information that she knew Phosa was looking for.

"Well, no, and yes. If any of you find yourself in trouble with your masters or need some shelter, leave Rome from the Portus Tiburtina. About two miles from the gate there is an old farming estate that has long been abandoned by my family. The original house is not there, but there is still a mud-brick shack that can be used as shelter. My servants come now and again to restock the supplies."

Phosa let out a deep breath. *That's a relief. At least there's a place to go...*

"But, I will warn you. If any of you ever needs this place, God forbid, it will only be open to you for a brief period of time as a safe house." Nevermind. Phosa's whole body had become numb, sitting in the same position on their cold tiled floor for at least an hour. She needed to get up to stretch. The group continued to talk amongst themselves, drink the last of the wine, and eat the last of their fish and bread.

As the sun fully disappeared below the horizon, the room was left in darkness. The stars and full moon outside provided some illumination, but it wasn't enough to light up the entire space. Phosa noticed this first and was busy replacing the candles and oil lamps.

"All right, thank you all for joining us here. We all know that as the night sky gets darker, the streets of Rome become filled with harsh truths and unfriendly people roaming about."

Phena extended a hand to help Fortuna and Linus up from their places on the couch. "Come on, up you go!"

"Don't bother with cleaning up; I'll get Phosa to take care of it later." She chuckled.

"What?"

"Hush, I'm kidding."

"Phena, could I speak with you by the door for a moment?" Junia asked graciously.

"Yes, of course."

"Come quickly!" Now, she sounded more agitated.

Phena rushed towards the front door and knelt down to look at a small, thin, folded square of paper on the floor. It looks like someone had silently slid the letter under the apartment door. She opened the paper, and feeling that it was important for them to know what it said sooner rather than later, she passed it to Junia to read. "What does it say?" Phena asked eagerly as she stood by. By now, the rest of the guests had realized there was a problem.

It says, "Run!"

chapter five
RUN!

Another warning. This is real now.

"Run, that's all it says?" Phena asked, looking at the paper.

"Yes, that's all it says," Junia assured her.

Phosa closed her eyes for a moment and took a deep breath. She knew what she had to do. *Jesus, protect me.* Phena opened the door quickly with one forceful swing, hoping to catch the messenger as he or she descended into the open courtyard below the balcony. There was no sign of anyone around. But what she did see and smell filled her with terror: bellowing smoke and a raging fire!

"Everyone out! Quickly!" She yelled into her apartment at the ten people that were still in there. They stood motionless, staring at her as if she had lost her mind.

"Let's go! There's a fire! We need to get out!" Junia shouted in desperation.

"Yes, let's go!" Phena motioned towards the door, and they listened, quickly exiting the apartment one by one. Phosa hastily gathered a few items she needed, stuffing them into her bag. She made sure to grab Paul's letter, some food, and a couple of tunics before the bag was full.

"Phena, Phosa! Look!" Junia pointed out the window, her eyes frantic. Phosa rushed across the room, brushing past those who were fleeing, and leaned out the same window. The sight before her was almost unbelievable. The streets outside their apartment building were filled with a seething mass of people, men, women, and even children, all shouting and jostling in a frenzy of anger and hatred. Their shouts were a confused muddle of words, but she could make out the general message. Phosa thought she might throw up or, worse, faint.

"They're accusing us of starting this, aren't they?"

"Let's go, sister! We have to get out of here." Phena roughly pulled her away from the window and towards the door that was now blackened and cracked. Phosa couldn't see Junia anywhere. "Where is Junia?"

"She must be out! Go!" Phena shouted, pulling her sister through the door and down the smoke-filled hallway. The tiled floor was hot to the touch, and scattered debris made an already difficult trail almost impossible to pass. Sensing that her sister was getting tired, Phosa resisted her prodding.

"Sister, I'm ok." But she didn't look so good. Her face was reddened with the heat, her eyes blinking furiously in defense of the smoke and ash all around them. Suddenly, she stopped, bent over, and coughed weakly.

"Go! I...I'll.." She fell to the ground, unconscious.

Phosa's eyes were wide with panic and filled with tears, frantically blinking against the thick smoke and ash that engulfed them. She stopped, doubled over, and coughed weakly. The heat was unbearable, and weakness took her. The crackling of flames and the shouts of angry voices outside filled the air. She was sure she had to be dreaming. This wasn't really happening. Flames were everywhere around her, but she did not feel their heat. The colors before her mingled with one another.

 Then she saw a dark figure with broad but slumped shoulders and a long flowing pallium fell to his knees. He was coming closer. His mouth was moving, but she could hear nothing but the distant murmur of, *"Incendiariae!"* and *"vapulabis!"*

Then darkness invaded.

"Phosa! Phosa! Wake up!" She heard the sound of a male voice and felt her body shake. She tried to open her eyes. Nothing.

"Phosa! Come on. I've got your sister!" She breathed in deeply and was immediately suffocated by deadly smoke. Her eyes recovered. There was a dark figure of a man before her. He had something heavy on his shoulders. She couldn't quite make out who it was. She recognized his voice.

"Phosa!" This time, his voice was louder and even more urgent. Rusticus. *It's Rusticus.* Phosa pushed herself up, the air thick with smoke and the heat pressing in around them. With Rusticus' strong support, she slung Phena's other arm over her shoulder, and together, they staggered down the hallway towards the flight of stairs.

"We must reach the courtyard!" Hurry!" Rusticus shouted from ahead of her, looking back towards her every now and again. Her tired body struggled to keep up. All around them, the building was buckling, its wooden frame bending like a fragile twig.

"Phosa! You must hurry!" He shouted,

waiting at the top of the staircase that led to the stoney courtyard, Phena's still unconscious body dangled dangerously over the edge. She heard the deafening sound of something crashing and felt a fresh blaze threaten to consume her. The beams were failing. Thick wooden strapping from the ceiling hung precariously from its place. She looked above Rusticus' head and realized that the cross beam that was keeping the second floor in place was barely holding.

"Rusticus! Move! You have to-" But it was too late. At that very moment, the building gave way, and the cross beam snapped, crushing Rusticus' shoulders. Phosa could only watch in horror as he and Phena tumbled down the stone staircase. She hurried to the bottom of the stairs, dreading what she might find. Her sister lay motionless on the floor, her limbs twisted at odd angles, and her eyes closed tight in unconsciousness.

She shifted her focus to her faithful servant, who was still awake but struggling to catch his breath. She could tell he was trying to say something, but no noise was coming out. And the infiltrating uproar of the mob outside wasn't helping.

She heard the angry cries of the crowd outside, shouting, "*Canes sordidae!*" Phosa desperately tried to drown out the angry cries of the crowd swarming the streets. "Phhoooss--ah!" Rusticus barely whispered. Phosa leaned in closer to him, secretly praying he would not die there in her arms. "Phhosa!"

"Yes, I'm here." She gently touched his head and felt a gapping bloody wound on the back of his head.

"Issss. Iss it— Bad?" He let out a full breath of air as if every word was a battle.

"Oh Rusticus." She didn't have the heart to be honest with him. "I... I'm no doctor."

"It's ok, miss Phosa! It was worth it! It's a fine way to die!"

"What? No! No! You're not going to die. Tears freely flowed down her face. He came back for us, and now this is what he gets? No!"

"You're going to be fine. Rusticus. We'll just call a doctor and..."

"Miss, you'll never drag me out of here. It's ok. Tend to those you can save!" He struggled to catch his breath, then closed his eyes.

Breathless and shaking, She was lost in the storm of her emotions. She touched Rusticus' hand, feeling the warm and sticky blood, and pressed a tender kiss onto his forehead, her determination to save them both growing stronger with each passing second. But the prospect of salvation was becoming more distant. The five-story structure directly in front of them had mostly collapsed into a giant pile of rubble. She was sure that if any of her neighbors remained on the floors above, they would have perished by now. Their only salvation had been this open-to-the-air courtyard.

"Exite huc!" [Come out here,] The angry crowd shouted from the other side of the archway.

"Te Iuppiter dique omnes perdant!" [jupiter and all the gods damn you!']

She fell to the ground, the smoke inhabiting her lungs. *God have mercy on us!* She prayed, fresh tears pouring down her face, forming a wet-dusty mixture. Suddenly, she caught the sound of her sister's harsh, raspy breathing. "Phosa?" *Hallelujah!*

Phosa rushed over to her sister, who was now sitting up and pulled her close. "Phena! Oh Phena!" She kissed her smokey hair and forced her sister to look at her. "Are you ok? Oh God, I thought I'd lost you!"

The taunts of the angry mob were getting ever louder and closer. *"Vestrae summae propudia!"* [you public scandal] Intermittently, she heard the sound of clay pots breaking against their shattered apartment building.

"Scelestae! Hoc insulae aedificium comburetis, et vos comburemimus!" [Scum! You burn this apartment block, and we'll burn you!"]

"Vigiles! Sunt incendiariae!" [police, there are arsonists about]

"Phosa, the building..."

"Yes, we have to get out of here."

"Incendiariae!"

"V*apulabis!"* [you're in for a whipping]

"What do I hear...?" Phena asked weakly.

"People, lots of people outside. They're angry"

Phosa put her arm around her sister and walked her towards the exit. And the mob.
"Phosa? Is Rusticus ok?"
"Sister, I don't think he's going to make it." Phosa looked over her shoulder. He was still lying there. His eyes closed. He looked dead.

"What? No?! Were you just going to leave him? We can't do that!" Phena suddenly shot herself up from the cement floor. "I'm not leaving him. Someone outside will help us. They have to."

By now there were even more people standing outside the burning building, some there to help and some to condemn. The chaos outside pierced through the crackling of flames- screams of concern from older women and accusations from men thrown at them by what sounded like an angry mob ready to pounce on them. With every ounce of strength she had, Phosa pulled her sister to the door, out the gate, and onto the street, and fell at the feet of the very people who were still jeering at them.

Breathless and in shock, the two sisters sat down, unable to move or speak after the disaster. Their angry voices faded into a somber silence. Phosa could sense their intense gaze fixed upon them, analyzing every move and waiting for an opportunity to strike. *Rusticus is still in there.*

She scanned the growing crowd, desperately seeking a familiar face. Maybe a member of their house church was still lingering. But she could not find even one kind face amongst them.

"Help! We need help! Our friend is still in there!"

"We'll not help the likes of you!" One hostile stranger shouted from within the mob.

"Please! I beg of you..."

"You probably meant for him to burn!"

"You want us to burn with him! *Incendiariae!*"

"*Incendiariae!*" "*Incendiariae!*" The crowd thundered in a renewed frenzy of murderous rage. Phosa stepped forward, her voice cutting through the chaos like a sharpened blade. "No! You don't understand," she shouted above the clamor, her tone firm and resolute. "We did not wish harm upon anyone. Please, hear us out!"

But the mob seemed deaf to reason, their shouts drowning out any attempt at explanation. Phosa's mind raced with fear and worry. How could she make them see the truth? Desperation fueled her next words as she implored, "Listen! Rusticus... he--" Before she could finish her sentence, a sudden commotion erupted in the distance. The sound of hurried footsteps and raised voices grew louder.

"You two!" Shouted a tall and skinny man with a nasty-looking burn on his arm.

She recognized him as one of their neighbors from the ground floor.

"Did you start the fire?"

"What?" Phosa could barely hear the man over the raging sea of tormented shouts surrounding her.

"Did you start it? We all know you host big gatherings. Perhaps one of your 'guests' was clumsy or overdrunk on the blood of your Lord?" Fear shot through Phosa's body. *Overdrunk? Is that what people think of us?* Phosa felt her sister's tight grip on her wrist. *She heard it, too.*

His loud and incriminating voice was attracting the attention of the onlookers crowding the streets. "Please, we are just..."

"Just what?"

"We didn't start the fire."

"Let's let the aedituus decide, shall we?" he said with a nasty smile that revealed his blackened teeth. The onlookers nodded their heads and roared their agreement, each one proclaiming both sisters' guilt.

"What should we do?" Phosa whispered to her sister.

"I don't know...there's nowhere to go!"

"And where did all your guests go? Ran from the scene, I see."

"They ran from a burning building as anyone would."

Unexpectedly, the man whipped his hand against Phosa's flesh; her cheeks burned with pain at the impact.

"I have nothing left because of you!"

"Yeah!" Came an angry yell from the circle of men.

"*Domum meam incendis!*" [What were you doing, anyway?]

"An official meeting of your cult, wasn't it?"

"Phosa, her sister nudged her closer, her voice still cracked by the smoke. "We have to get out of here."

"Whispering now, eh?" *She's right. They're going to kill us. We have to run.*

Mumbling a prayer under her breath, Phosa grabbed her sister's hand and with her head down as a shield, she roughly pushed through the crowd. Then when they were free of the mob, they ran like they'd never run before towards Via Lata. She had a plan, but it was risky,. She needed to get to Porta Tiburtina and quickly! Pulling her still groggy sister along, they passed carts as they pounded down the streets with their wares, foul-smelling oxen, and constantly braying donkeys whipped for their service.

Head down, Phosa continued to run past open-air pubs and brothels, refusing to satisfy her curiosity by looking inside. She made her next turn onto Via Labicana and then shortly again onto Via Nomentana. They still had another twenty minutes to go until they were rid of the city of Rome. Phosa quickly looked back to see how her sister was faring. Phena's shoulders were slumped with exhaustion, and her face was ashen grey. Overcome with guilt and worry, Phosa slides into a side street, out of the public eye, and lets go of her sister. Phena immediately fell to the ground in a coughing fit. Overcome, she was amazed her sister had made it that far.

"Phhoosa! I can't!" Another coughing fit interrupted her.

"It's ok. We'll just sit here for a few minutes."

"Phosa?"

"Yes?" She answered, shifting herself closer to her sister and pulling this unfamiliarity frail creature towards her.

"Thank you!" Phosa smiled and took her first full breath of air in what seemed like an eternity of horror. *You're welcome.*

Phosa's eyes opened in a flash, and immediately, the pain in her neck was too much for her to bear. She hadn't meant to fall asleep. She could hear the muffled sound of angry men shouting, but couldn't tell if that was just a memory. Then she heard the unmistakable sound of metal clanging against metal and the individual stomp of leather against the road. *They're coming for us.*

"Phena!" She whispered, gently jabbing her sister's shoulder. "Phena, wake up! They're coming!" Phosa helped her still sleepy sister to her feet, the dull ache of her neck turning into shooting pain. "Let's go!" Phosa took her sister's hand again and ventured back onto the streets in the direction of Porta Tiburtina. She knew the gate was close.

"Phosa, where are you taking us?" Phena asked, hobbling along behind her. "And what about Rusticus?"*Rusticus! ....But if we go back... Going back would mean facing certain death, but staying on this uncertain path was no better.*

Phosa bravely looked her sister in the eyes,and held her hand tightly their fingers intertwined. "We have to keep going. Our friend is now in God's hands." To Phosa's utter horror, Phena shrugged off her grip and stopped abruptly, the sound of metal still clanging in the distance.

"That's it? You're seriously ok with just leaving him there?" *No of course not!* She thought to herself but knew if she wanted to live, there was no other choice. They had to keep running.

The sound of marching boots was getting closer. And with it, their doom.

 "Keep your voice down, sister! You're usually the reasonable one in these situations! You know if we go back there, we will die!"

"Maybe that's our fate!"

"No! It can't be! We were saved from the fire! We must keep going!"

Phosa tried to grab onto her sister again "For what? What do we have to keep going for?"

"It is God's will!"

"Is it God's will for Rusticus to die?" Phosa couldn't allow herself to go there. She wanted to live. This time, she used a force she didn't know she had.

"You asked me where I'm taking you. To the Porta Tiburtina."

chapter six
NO WHERE ELSE TO GO

Phosa bent over to catch her breath, and Phena followed suit. She inspected her partially burned sandals and bruised feet, blistered by their frantic journey. They had been running so fast and for so long that she had lost track of where they were. Although she was sure she'd passed through this way with her father a number of times, she could recognize nothing in the darkness. The streets around them were quiet. About a decade before, Claudius devoted their route to military use only, but since his ascension to the throne, Nero had limited its use. It was said he complained of too many gates to maintain in the city. And for once, this decree of Nero's was to their advantage.

Their journey took them along Via Tiburtina and then through the imposing stone gate that had been built to protect Rome from barbarians. Its tall, vacant towers rose high above their heads. The way was open to them, and they walked through it, hoods raised and eyes forward. Phosa remembered Junia's words but hadn't expected that they'd come in handy so soon. Earlier that evening, she had mentioned the location of a safe house—just two miles outside the Tiburtina. Two miles and then safety.

Attached to the gate was a length of cement wall that stretched for as far as the eye could see. There were also a few gatehouses and storefronts on either side of the road butting up to the city gates, but they looked abandoned. The scent of mildew and decay lingered in the air, a musty reminder of the buildings' neglect. Phosa also caught a whiff of something metallic, like old blood.

As they passed by, Phosa thought she saw little eyes peering out at her, watching as she and her sister passed by. Her need for a bed outweighed her curiosity.

"We've passed the Porta Tiburtina, sister. Now, where are we going?"

"Were you not listening?" Phosa asked, enjoying being in the know for once.

"It's been a long day..." Phena returned impatiently, dragging her feet as she walked slowly behind her.

"Junia mentioned a safe house. I'm taking you there." Expecting gratitude, she only received silence. She swallowed her bitterness and kept walking. The road was a morbid path of concrete, lined with the forgotten graves of generations past, while beyond stretched the fruitful fields of life, a stark contrast to the decay behind them.

She looked on either side of the road for signs of a farm estate. Then she saw it. A large rectangular villa standing just a quarter mile from the road. It stood tall and majestic, made of sturdy concrete and covered in a faded cream-colored plaster. The roof was topped with red clay tiles now full of overgrown vegetation.

Phena was the first to leave the road and venture onto the path towards the villa. Phosa could see her steps were marked by a new determination. "Do you see the shack?"

"It's there." Phena pointed towards a small cement building off to the right that had a simple stable attached and several large vessels stored against it.

She inhaled deeply, and a sense of relief flooded through her. Phosa hurried through the abandoned field to catch up with her sister, who was approaching the shack.

Phosa wiped away cobwebs and dust from the surface of the glass windows, and peered into the lifeless building.

"Is it safe?"

"No, but we have nowhere else to go."

ONE MONTH LATER

Phosa woke up from her nightmare with a loud, piercing scream She sat up, her heart racing, sweat clinging to her skin. The room was dimly lit by the early morning sun filtering in through the dusty windows. Beside her, Phena's bed of straw was empty. With shaky hands, Phosa pushed aside the thin blanket covering her and lifted herself up to her feet. She tiptoed towards the door, the floorboards creaking softly under her weight. As she reached for the latch, a knot of fear twisted in her stomach. *Where is Phena?!*

The door burst open, revealing her sister amidst a group of children. They were all caked in dirt and dressed in minimal clothing as they played in the mud.

"Phosa! Good morning!" Her sister smiled pleasantly, "Did you sleep ok? I thought I heard you scream a second ago."

"Sorry, I..."Phosa felt her forehead, wondering if it was really spinning or if she just felt like it was.

"Did you have the same nightmare?"About Rusticus?"

"Yes, but I don't want to talk about it."

“It might help to talk..”

“Sister, he haunts me in my dreams. I can still see his body just lying there.”

“Ok, ok, don’t give me nightmares!”

“Don’t you ever think about it? And him?”

“Of course I do, but we can’t change what happened. He chose to save us.”

“Yes, and now we owe him everything.”

“Let’s make it count. First, eat. I’ve foraged for some herbs, nuts, and berries.” She heard the sound of tiny fingers tapping on the front door.

“The children will eat with us!” Phena’s long hair brushed her face as she walked past her into their shack again, and four children followed. Phosa wasn’t very good at figuring out how old children were, but she guessed that the oldest one was about ten and the youngest, who looked particularly frail was about three.

The oldest child, a girl with short brown hair, an olive complexion, and a drenched glare, took on the mothering role and guided the younger children to the table. For small children, they behaved rather well.

“I want some oats!” The youngest girl asked, whose name was Festia.

“How do you say that politely?” the oldest girl asked her in her most authoritative mothering tone.

“Please, Sari? Oh, please?” The girl smiled, already handing the little girl a bowl of food. Phena watched from the side table and prepared dishes for the two boys who were patiently waiting outside.

Their shack was already crowded, with just two people in it.

After the children finished, they went back outside to play. Phena dutifully wiped the half-broken wood table, which was one of the only pieces of furniture that they had, and cleaned the wooden bowls in the bucket of water she'd retrieved from the well. She then picked up the broom and started to sweep away the remnants of breakfast. They'd managed to straighten up the old shack since arriving to the point where it was almost comfortable. Still, it was a meager existence with a corner for their straw beds, a table to eat at with two precariously unstable wooden chairs, and a small oven in the corner to keep warm and make meals, with a scant cabinet of basic cooking supplies. They found some linens, blankets, curtains, and even a rug from the old abandoned villa on the same property.

"You know, we'd be able to entertain a lot easier if we just occupied that huge villa over there," Phosa mentioned for the twentieth time, this time more sarcastically, knowing what her sister's response would be. Lately, she'd spent quite some time daydreaming about living in such a villa, a brood of laughing children all around her, with the strong, loving arms of her husband wrapped firmly around her waist. It was a welcome reprieve from her guilt of leaving Rusticus.

"We've discussed this Phosa. Junia offered the shack not the villa." Phena answered, as she motioned for the children to go back outside so she could sweep the shack. Phosa watched, not feeling awake enough to help.

"Don't you think it's strange that no one has come out here? Didn't she say her servants made regular trips?"

"Someone will come. I'm sure of it."

"And why are you sure, sister?"

"What if we've been sending letters to no one? What if Junai didn't make it out of that fire!!" Phosa didn't intend to raise her voice at her sister, but she couldn't restrain her emotions any longer. The floodgates had opened, and she couldn't stop now.

"Would we even know if she didn't? Who would tell us? Who, Phena? We are out here alone! Alone!" Tears streamed down Phosa's face as the stark reality of their situation hit her. With everything, she wanted to fight back the hopelessness that she felt, but she didn't know how. And Phena didn't understand. Phosa gently laid her head on the freshly wiped table and sobbed.

"Phosa?" Her sister's voice was gentle and calm. Not at all what she expected.

"Yes?" Phosa heard the sound of the broom being laid against the wooden wall of the shack and then felt the soothing touch of her sister's delicate hand on her shoulder. For the first time in a very long time, she was grateful she at least had her sister.

"Phosa, we are not alone. We have each other, and we have our faith. Junia is resourceful; she will find a way to reach out to us. We must trust in that."

Phosa lifted her tear-streaked face from the table, her eyes meeting her sister's. She had no more words to say and could see by the look on her sister's face that they weren't necessary. With a deep breath, Phosa sat up in her chair, wiping away her tears with the back of her hand.

"You're right, Phena. We have to trust that Junia will find a way to reach us. We can't lose hope."

"That's right. We always have each other. And more importantly, no matter what destitution or danger we face we'll always have our faith. No one can take that away."

Phena smiled, caringly rubbed her back, and then walked out the door to check on the children.

Her renewed sense of well-being brought on hunger pains, and she only just realized that she hadn't had any breakfast. She spooned herself some oatmeal that was still sitting in the pot on the stove and then went to the window to watch her sister and the children. A grin spread across Phosa's face as she watched the children line up and take their turns catching a ball that Phena was throwing. The sun shone down, highlighting the dust particles in the air and the worn fabric of the children's clothing. Phosa felt a pang of guilt and sadness as she watched the children, some with bare feet, standing on the dirt ground. This is all they've known. And still, they seem grateful. Even happy. Phosa resolved to do better. Be better. And wait.

Phosa turned from the window and ate her breakfast at the table. The joyful banter and happy squeals of the children, as they enjoyed their simple game, brought peace to Phosa's soul. Just as she was scrapping the last of her oatmeal from her wooden bowl, she noticed that all was silent. Phena had vanished, and the children had vanished. Phosa got up from her spot on the bed and peered out the window. She spotted Phena at the well near the villa. Relieved, she pulled off her sweat-stained tunic and put on a clean one that had been hanging in their house overnight. She strapped her bag around her shoulder, placed her feet in her battered sandals, and went to meet her sister.

As she made her way across the wide field towards the well, she couldn't shake off the unsettling sensation of being watched. She refused to turn around and look back at her small shack or towards the road behind her, too afraid of who might notice her.

Even though this stretch of the Appian Way was not often travelled by the general public, there were still daily visitors and mourners at the tombs that dotted the road. All it would take is for one person to spot her and then...

The well was closer to the villa than the shack and shaded by a nearby olive grove. It was a simple-looking round brick structure with the usual curved top and pulley system. Not far from the well, she could hear the gentle sound of the underground spring that fed the well its fresh water. Phena was bent over the opening, her long flowing hair covering her face.

Phosa approached her sister cautiously, not wanting to startle her. She waited until her sister had finished retrieving the bucket from the depths below.

“Phena?”

“Sister, help me with this bucket, will you?”

“Phena, what is our plan?”

“For today? Well, I need you to write a letter.”

“No, I mean...”

“Listen, I can’t do it, so you have to.” Phena straightened up, wiping the sweat from her brow with the back of her hand. She looked up at Phosa with a mix of exhaustion and determination. Phosa nodded, understanding that her sister was trying to keep their spirits up.

They returned to their shack with two fresh buckets of water. Phena carefully poured some into a bowl for feet washing and then poured the rest of hers into the pot that was on the fire. Phosa got out her writing materials and took a seat at the table. “Ok, what...who is the letter for? And are we sending it the same way we did the others? That hasn’t really been working, has it?”

"I hadn't really thought of that yet. One step at a time, sister. Please write to Junia."

"So, what do you want me to say? Are you going to give me the words?" Phosa couldn't contain her annoyance. She really wanted to hurl the bottle of ink onto the floor. And give up.

"Phosa, there's no sense getting upset. And I thought we already talked about this."

"I'm not upset. I'm just-"

"Just what...?"

"Ok, fine, I'm upset. I'm still upset. I can't keep living like this. With no hope! I mean, it was only a month ago that you asked me why we should go on...."

Phena turned her head, avoiding eye contact as if she felt embarrassed to hear her own words being thrown back to her.

"We always have hope, sister. God saved us from the fire. Do you think he saved us so we could die here?"

"I hope not!"

"Well, He didn't. He has a plan. And I think I'm beginning to understand what that could be."

chapter seven
JUNIA'S VILLA

Phosa placed her stylus back in its frame. "I need some air."

"The door's right there."

"Sister, I need to know what your plan is. How long do you expect me to live in this dirty, grimy old slave's shack?"

"We have food. We have shelter. What more do you want?"

Rage surged through Phosa's body, making every muscle taut. How does she not understand? "I want A life! A husband! A future, sister!" Her voice rose to a yell.

"The stench in this place is unbearable! And Junia hasn't answered our five letters!" Phosa's head dropped onto the table as tears streamed down her face. Phosa's sobs echoed in the small room, the only sound besides the creaking of the floorboards and the distant sounds of city life. As she inhaled, the putrid odor of must and decay saturated her senses.

"Phosa, look at me." Phena prodded gently. She didn't listen. She couldn't meet her sister's calm gaze. "Do you think God can only take care of us inside the walls?"

I hate when she does this! "No..."

"Well, then-?" Phena was interrupted by the sound of the children shrieking outside. Phena smiled and looked out the window. The children had returned.

"The little one is climbing again, isn't she?"

"She's a persistent one. I don't blame her; those pears are really good!" Just the other day, Phosa caught a vision of the little one attempting to climb up the pear tree just outside their door. She had to admit that they were really cute and was happy for the distraction they provided.

"I should really help her. Can you please write that letter?"

"Yes. I asked Junia to send word and food again. Hopefully, this time, someone will answer."

"She will. I'm sure of it! Could you add a postscript that I'd like Decius to come? I have a question for him."

"I could, but don't you think Junia needs her accountant? What do you want him for?"

"I'll tell you when I tell him."

"Ok?" *Ominous as usual.*

"You know, sister, you should really try to have a little more faith in these things. God will provide. Things will be ok."

"How can I? Look around you!"

"Faith is the assurance of things hoped for..."

"Yes, and the conviction of things not seen, I know."

Everything inside of her wanted to get out of that cold, wet, dusty hole that had been their home for the past month. Maybe, against all odds, this would be the letter that would get through. As obedient as ever, she grabbed a long piece of red-dyed wool that she'd scavenged from the villa and wrapped it around her shoulders before she sat down on the wooden chair that somehow hadn't snapped after a month's worth of use.

Phosa loved writing. She loved the smell of the ink as it caressed the tip of the stylus and the small black puddle that inevitably fell from the pen onto the paper at impact. It was one of the few activities that brought her peace and relaxation. She could enter a world that she was creating for herself. Most often, that world did not have anything to do with her reality. *Perfect.*

Her father had always said that being able to read and write was both a privilege and a responsibility, and she felt it every time she picked up a pen. Sometimes, she wondered how her father dared to teach his daughter to read and write, and his youngest daughter at that. If she closed her eyes, Phosa could see her father, with his worn and calloused hands, bent over the clay codex, standing over her in the market stall, carefully marking each stroke with the stylus, keeping accounts, and writing letters to merchants. She could still hear his voice instructing her as he made the impressions on the clay.

Here, Phosa, you try!

She shook off her wandering thoughts and refocused on the task at hand. She began her letter with the customary greeting;

Phosa let out a deep breath. She couldn't help but be a little curious as to why her sister wanted to see this servant of Junia's. She had no idea who he was or how he might help. But it was a good sign that she was planning something. Phosa left the letter to dry on the table and went outside to get some air. She could no longer hear the shrieks of the hoard of children. They must have moved into the distant fields. *All the better that they did.*

She took advantage of the moment to search for any extra provisions in the villa that could come in handy for them. She had already taken everything useful from the scribe's room on the first floor; she was sure that there was much more to discover. She closed the decaying wooden door of their shack and pulled her hood over her hair. The sun blazed down over the open field, scorching the grass. She walked past the well and then up the stone walkway towards the front door of the villa. She slowly pushed the door open, ready for anything. But all she encountered was a sudden blast of dust. She coughed and lowered her head, making her way through the atrium of the house and towards the colonnaded hallway that led to the gardens in the back. She knew from her past visit that the kitchen was a very small room located just off of the hallway. She turned the corner and followed the faded symbols of bread and fish on the mosaic floors. Pushing open the creaking door to the kitchen, Phosa was met with a scene of abandonment. Cobwebs hung from the ceiling, and dust coated the countertops. The once vibrant heart of the villa's activity now stood frozen in time.

Her eyes fell on the clay jars lining the shelves. Perhaps there were still some provisions left behind. As she stood there, she couldn't help but wonder why Junia's family had left this place behind. In her mind's eye, she could envision the beauty it must have held in its prime. She carefully inspected each jar, hoping to find something that could sustain them for a while longer. She placed some glass containers of grains, flour, and nuts in her bag and continued on.

Then something caught her eye that hadn't the last time she came to the villa: a small mysterious door leading to the western wing of the villa.

She hadn't yet explored that section and was curious what she would find. She held onto the long, rusted metal handle of the door and lightly pushed. The wooden door gave way with barely a touch, its cracked frame held together by rusted hinges. The secret room in front of her was a simple wooden addition with a dirt floor. A strong, musty odor assaulted Phosa's senses as soon as she stepped into the room. It was a mixture of damp earth, rotten wood, and something unidentifiable but undoubtedly unpleasant. Tall shelves lined one side of the room, and a large circular stone structure was at the other end. *They must have employed their own baker.* She thought, still holding a hand to her nose.

If she closed her eyes, she could still smell the mix of freshly baked bread and salt. Unfortunately, whoever had closed up this room had taken everything of value with them. Phosa was about to leave the baker's shop when she spotted something behind the long wooden bench to the left of the door. There was a small clay bowl full of a white sandy substance. Is that salt? If it was salt, she knew that it could be sold for a small fortune. She quickly grabbed the bowl and left.

Phosa set the bowl carefully inside her bag. She left the baker's shop and the kitchen and returned to the fresh air of the hallway and garden. *OK, now let's find some more clothes and blankets.* She wandered down the hall, opening all of the doors and inspecting the rooms. Most of them were simple servants' quarters, completely empty save for a stone slab where the mattress used to be. After finding nothing of use in any of the other rooms, she inspected the last room at the end of the hall. This one was larger than the rest and painted in richly colored frescos that were mostly faded. The scene looked like a group of women relaxing together by the river, with several servants about them.

In the room, there was a loom set up and a shelf full of materials and dies. The loom still had a half-completed cloth on it with an intricate and unique triangle design. *Why would anyone leave this half-completed?* On the other side of the room, there was a shelf filled with light brown wool commonly used for plebian wear. She took two piles off the shelves and dusted them off. *These will wash nicely, I think.* Then she peered up at the other folded linens in an array of colors, ranging from bold reds to soft greens and even a luxurious blue fabric. The garments were expertly crafted with intricate embroidery and precise hemlines. Each piece looked like it would cost a small fortune! She was immediately drawn to the green cloth, which perfectly complemented her sage eyes. Without hesitation, she snatched up all of the green and also grabbed some red fabric that would suit Phena's complexion. Phosa envisioned herself draped in a luxurious stolla made of the radiant green fabric. *Now, we just need to find someone to take us in, and I'll have a line of men waiting for me to choose from!*

With determination burning in her mossy green eyes, Phosa made her way back to their makeshift shelter, clutching the precious materials close to her chest. The sun was beginning its descent in the sky, casting a warm glow over the dilapidated villa and the surrounding fields. Phena's sandals were not by the front door, indicating that she was still out. This was a relief to Phosa; she wasn't sure how Phena would react to her taking the material without permission.

chapter eight
A NEW CALLING

Phena had to agree that she was warmer now that the stolen wool covered them during the cold December nights. But she still didn't like it. She didn't like the situation much more than Phosa did; she was just less vocal about her complaints.

And it wasn't the sudden poverty that made her anxious, fearful, or down. No, she could handle sleeping on the dusty floor of their confiscated shack. She could handle eating mostly bread and drinking only watered-down wine. She could stand walking around in her old sun-stained and cracked leather sandals, that she would have gotten rid of months ago if she had anything else to wear.

What she couldn't stand was having nothing to do, no mission for her life, and no purpose. She couldn't stand wondering if God had rejected them and decided that they weren't meant to serve fellow brothers and sisters as she thought they were. She couldn't stand living with the possibility that God had even cursed them for leaving behind their servant to die a terrible, fiery death. The bleakness of such a thought consumed her until she felt like she couldn't breathe. "God, have mercy on me and my sister." She prayed aloud and immediately felt the compression in her throat loosen.

She could never go back to the way her life used to be before she found Christ. But these days outside the city were bringing her dangerously closer to her life without Jesus. They were pointless and meaningless. And that type of life only leads to drunkenness, thievery, and desperation. That alone gave her anxiety.

Phosa will never understand any of this. She's only concerned with our material welfare. She didn't seem to care that they no longer had a mission, a way of serving others, a calling. The only comfort Phena could find was in the evenings, when Phosa lay fast asleep next to her, and she burned their oil lamp late into the night so that she could pray. While she couldn't read Paul's letters like Phosa could, Phena still found solace in praying. She spent hours on her knees, pleading with Jesus for guidance and a clear path forward. Her heart longed for a new mission, a sense of purpose reigniting within her.

It was on one particularly dark and cold December evening that she wrapped herself up in the stolen wool blankets and sat at the table with her head bowed. She'd done this night after night ever since their escape from Rome. Desperate to hear even just one word of comfort from her Lord and Savior, Phena was resolved to be honest. "Lord, I have served you with fervent passion since the day I first believed. And I only seek to continue with my service. Would you give me an opportunity? Even if it brings me nothing but poverty and strife. I only wish to know you are with me.
She begged, "Please, Lord, speak to me."

But there was only silence. She sat as still as a statue, and the only sound in the room was her sister's soft snoring. And then she heard it —a firm but gentle voice.
Look outside. It said to her. Phena rose from her seated position at the table and stepped outside of their hovel. The crickets were playing their usual evening tune, and the white-yellow moon was shining brightly in the cloudy night sky.

Listen. It said to her. She quieted herself and focused. She could hear the sound of several small children laughing in the distance. It was the orphan children who lived in another abandoned building about a mile down the road.

"Yes, I hear the children." She silently replied to her Lord. *Help my children!*

With a soft smile gracing her lips, Phena took a deep breath and turned back towards the hovel, her mind ablaze with purpose. The Lord had shown her the answer she'd been seeking, and now it was up to her to act on it. She knelt down on her straw mattress, a smile still on her lips. As she was drifting off to sleep, she was somewhat startled to see Daria, one of the orphaned children, peering in through their window. But her sweet and inquisitive expression reminded her again of her God-given mission. *Help my children!*

The next morning, as the first rays of sunlight filtered through the cracks in the walls of their humble hovel, Phena woke up with a renewed sense of purpose. Her heart was brimming with excitement but also burden knowing the risks she would have to take. Still, she wanted to tell Phosa, but she knew it wasn't the right time yet. They needed Junia's help before they could move forward. Five, now six letters and no response. She was beginning to wonder if something was wrong.

Did Junia get any of their letters? If she did, why didn't she respond? And if she didn't, then we are all in grave danger. Phosa didn't hold anything back in those letters! She named them Christians. And that was enough to seal their fate and send them into the shadows where only lions would find them. In her mind's eye, she could see vultures circling their prey. Her hands began to tremble, and her chest quaked under each beat of her heart. In the corner of the room, Phosa's sleeping body jostled in her bed as she muttered something. *Keep it together Phena!*

Vultures still circling, she knew that everything depended on those letters being received by the right people. Phena sat in the candlelite darkness for hours, contemplating their danger, bringing herself to a calmer resolve. It was only after the sun had fully penetrated their hovel, that Phosa finally rose from her bed.

"You're up early," She said sleepily.

"Not really." Phena grinned at her enchanting sister; her hair was sticking straight up, and her face contorted as if she had just drank too much sour wine. She stretched her arms up and then hobbled to the table where Phena was sitting.

"I hate to be a bother, sister…"

"What?" Phosa moaned.

"Did you send the letter you wrote yesterday?"

"Yes, the same way we did the others."

"Excellent!"

Phena paced restlessly back and forth across the short fare of their shack, all the while fiddling with one of the only possessions she cared for: her mother's gold bangle. She'd always wondered where her mother got it from, knowing that her background was dubious. She twisted the bangle around and around her wrist, hoping it would keep her mind from their predicament.

"Ok, so you walked to the gate and placed it in the hole like I said?"

"Yes."

"Then why hasn't he come yet?"

"How should I know?"

Phena let out a moan of frustration and would have left their small house if the warmth from their oven was not such a comfort to her. The weather had taken a turn, and now their shack was even less comfortable. Even she wondered how much longer they could live outside the city. *There has to be something else we can do. We're just waiting around to die out here.* Phena's anxious pacing quickly devolved into frenzied circular movements, causing her to become dizzy. Then she noticed her sister had gotten out a piece of parchment.

"What are you writing? To whom?" Phena asked, hearing the eagerness in her own voice as she bent over her sister's shoulders. "Are you asking for more food?"

"Sister, why do you hunch over me as if you could read what I'm writing? You know you can't."

Her sister's words clawed at her like a savage animal. She took a seat at the table opposite her sister. *How could she be so cruel?*

"I just want to know who you're writing to."

"I'm not writing to anyone. I'm copying one of Paul's letters." All at once, her heart was lightened by the mention of Paul, but she felt envious of her sister's ability to support their brothers and sisters even from afar and in poverty. Her father had taught her younger sister how to read and write but hadn't thought it important to do the same for her. She couldn't figure out why he would do that. And why Phosa? What did he think she would do with such a talent? Her concerns were on material things and the here and now: getting married, having children, eating good food, and wearing fine clothes. *Come on, Phena, that's not fair.* She thought to herself. *Phosa is copying Paul's letters. That's a good thing. I should be proud of her.*

Phena quietly asked her forgiveness. The poisonous drip of her jealousy worried her.

Her mind drifted back to what was before her. Her sister's eyes were locked on hers. And her mouth was moving. "Phena?"

"I'm ok, sister."

With nothing else to say, Phena wrapped one of the wool blankets around her shoulders and stepped outside.

"Where are you going?"

"To see the children."

She walked out the door and a few minutes into the surrounding fields until she reached an easily memorable tree that served as a marker for the children's hideout. It was a huge bulk of a tree that surpassed all others in height. The children were very clever. They had constructed an elaborate system of grass-covered hideaways using some old pieces of lumber that they'd found in the abandoned market stalls. Phena quietly walked up to the place where she knew the first hatch was hidden. She bent over and knocked thrice on the grassy exterior of the main door.

"Hello? Pueri, It's me, Phena." Suddenly, the wooden trap door dislodged itself from the grassy surface, and the small and innocent face of a little girl emerged. She had long dark brown hair that reached to her waist, golden green eyes, and a mischievous smirk on her dust-encrusted face.

"What's the magic password?"

"Magic password? I uh, I don't think anyone told me."

She leaned forward and whispered, "just say any word."

"Any word?"

"Yes, go on!"

"Fortuna" *Why that word?*

The little girl turned her face away from Phena for a moment and whispered the word to the ground. Presumably, another child was just below her and was helping her to evaluate Phena's case.

"Yes, that will do. Watch your step."

Phena did as she was told and descended into the children's cleverly built hiding place. Below the ground was a hollowed-out rock-faced structure in the shape of a rectangle. The room was not big, but it didn't need to be as three small tunneled paths led to additional rooms.

"This is impressive!"

"Yes, we are lucky. The orphans of Rome may not have anything of value, but our resourcefulness."

For some reason, Phena didn't like the sound of that. Orphans shouldn't have to be resourceful. They should be taken care of by adults who care about them. The children carried torches with them that gave the tunnels a light glow to them but were insufficient, to say the least. Phena counted five shadows of children just sitting up against the rock walls playing with rocks and sticks and whatever else they could find on the surface.

"So, what do you want now?"

"What do you mean?"

"Well, you're here. Now what?"

"Oh, I just wanted to see where you live and how you survive out here."

"Then you'll want to meet Daria."

"Whose Daria?" Phena only a knew a handful of their names and Daria didn't ring a bell.

"She's our teacher. She's older than all the others. You'll probably want to see her."

"Yeah, I suppose I do."

"Ok, this way." The little girl went down on her hands and knees and started to crawl through one of the three tunnels. From what she could see, it led toward the southwest side of the city. *I wonder how intricate these tunnels are. And how many kids live down here...*

Phena placed all of her hope in this little girl's ability to get to Daria. The tunnels were cramped and had stale, recycled air wafting through them. Focusing intently, she could just make out the petite feet of the girl in front of her.

"How much further?"

"You'll see."

chapter nine

A FIXER-UPPER

The absence of her sister brought a quiet tension, like the silence before the storm, and a deep unease settled in her gut like an unwelcome guest. Unnerved, she went back to her copy work. Phosa tried to forget about it and get back to work. She'd already made three copies of Paul's most recent letter to the churches in Rome. She meant to keep going until she ran out of supplies. The thick scroll, given to her by Paul's messenger, lay open on the table. Its edges were slightly singed from the fire and their hasty escape.

The flickering flame of the gas lamp danced and cast shadows on the walls of the small room as Phosa started another copy. One hand lightly traced the words on the parchment, and the other her stylus gliding effortlessly over the fresh paper. The beauty of the words dripped from her stylus onto the fresh paper. She could almost feel the power of Paul's message as she wrote his words again and again. She had to admit to herself that before this exercise, she didn't know much about the great apostle. She could remember her sister talking about the apostle Paul and how he had been traveling all over the Mediterranean spreading the news of Jesus Christ and planting churches. He remained an aloft other-worldly figure, someone to be revered.

And now, someone that Phosa desperately wanted to meet. She had questions to ask him. The first section of Paul's letter to the brothers and sisters in Rome was simply a summary of what they believe as Christians. Phosa appreciated the reminder and the common ground that could be found in the words. As she transcribed, one particular sentence caught her attention."You are among those Gentiles who were called to belong to Jesus."

I am called to belong to Jesus. Like. He chose me? Even after I've done such wretched and horrible things? Phosa kept reading those words over and over. She hadn't felt like she belonged to anyone or anything ever since her father died. And even though she called herself a Christian for a few months now, she didn't quite feel part of the 'family' yet. Phena had always told her that they were both the leaders of their house church, but she didn't feel like a leader. *I mean, how could I when, most of the time, I feel lost and out of place?* She had no idea what other Christians were saying when they talked about baptism or being 'born again' or when they said The Holy Spirit lived inside of each believer. She had never read the other letters that Paul had written. She wished that there had been someone close to her who could have spoken to her about the deeper truths and mysteries of The Way. At the start, Junia had taught her whole family the basic teachings, but that was it. All she knew was that Jesus died on the cross for her sins and came back to life again and that she could, too, if she believed in him. That's all she knew. And it didn't make her feel like much of a leader. But Paul's letter said that she was meant to be a Christian. She was meant to turn away from her pagan life. So, she thought to herself, there must be so much more to learn.

Phosa's desk is cluttered with sheets of parchment, filled with scribbled notes and underlined passages. Hours and hours went by. As she read, her eyes grew wide with wonder and amazement at the words of Paul. She was amazed at his tone of authority; and at his confidence as he expressed the amazing truths that only a god could know.

After a while, she got up out of her chair to stretch out her stiff hand and to relieve her eyes of their daunting task. All of a sudden, Phosa's ears picked up a sound from outside that was not the usual chatter of Phena or children. She heard the voices of two men, and with every passing second, the voices were getting louder and louder.

Panic flooded through her as she frantically searched for a place to hide all of her work. With trembling hands, Phosa crept towards the open window of her meager hovel. She spotted two figures making their way through the fields, heading straight towards her dwelling. Heart racing, she quickly dropped to the floor, grabbing her important transcriptions as she did. *Lord, I need you again!* Phosa silently prayed to herself. Questions raced through her mind as she peered at the abandoned villa in the distance. Why were they going there? In all the months since she had been living outside the walls, no one had dared enter that property – until now. As the men approached the well and continued on towards the front door of the house, Phosa crouched below the window, straining to hear their movements and figure out their intentions. She left the safety of her shack, raised her hood, and quietly followed them. She made it to the well and hid behind its stone belly. The men were still outside, gazing at the exterior of the house.

"This is it."

"Looks like a fixer-upper."

The men did not have any uniforms to identify them. To the right stood a towering figure, adorned in a grass-green tunic cinched with a belt, and carrying a trade axe on his side. His hair was damp and light brown from perspiration. He had a large nose, and a rugged unshaven face. *Looks like a working man, that one.*

"Yeah, the last owner left in a hurry."

"Reason?"

"Criminal. That's what the paper says." Replied the man on the left, who held a wax codex that he would reference every few seconds and a stylus in his hand. Perhaps a scribe. His longer cream tunic with embroidered edges was much more respectable and didn't bear the tell-tale signs of hard labor.

"Criminal, eh? What was his crime?"

"He was a Christian. His whole family was."

The thumping of Phosa's heart echoed loudly in her ears, drowning out any other sound as she focused on the men's words.

"Ok, so let's take a look inside." the dirtier of the two men suggested. He walked up to the glass windows and peered in.

"The door might be difficult to open." warned the man with the codex. He walked over to the door, looking as if he was ready to knock it over with one shove of his hip. Instead of meeting resistance, the door swung wide open, and the man fell face-first into the house. Phosa suppressed a chuckle. The man who was still outside let out a roar of a laugh and said, "Should be difficult, eh? Ha!"

"It shouldn't have opened so easily. It's not been in use for over two years!" The scribe looked at the door and wiggled it, clearly suspicious of some foul play.

"If there's been looters, we are in a lot of trouble! You realize that, right, Atticus?"

"Yes, you don't need to remind me."

The men disappeared into the villa and Phosa didn't have the courage to follow. She closed her eyes and tried to think. If they were found, then they would likely be turned over to the censor.

They would be either taken as prostitutes or Christians, neither having a great chance of survival.

Ok, what do I do? What do I do? Phena would know exactly what to do! Panic set in as her eyes scanned the fields, willing Phena to return. But the fields were clear. She was alone. Phosa tried desperately to quiet herself and to regulate her breathing. *Think! Think!* She had to figure out what those men were doing. She took a few more deep breaths and peered out past the safety of the well. Maybe they left the door open. They did but had ventured to the back of the house, out of sight. *What could they be doing?* The one man looked like he was dressed like a man of a trade. *Maybe he's a builder? And the other man was much cleaner. Maybe he worked for the city?*

It was crucial that she found out the truth. Phosa took a deep breath and closed her eyes, trying to calm herself. She repeated the mantra in her head: *I am capable of this.* Just as she was about to stand up from her crouched position, a loud knocking sound coming from behind her made her jump and sent her back into a state of fear. The knock turned into a pound. And another. She bravely turned around to catch a glimpse of the one doing the pounding.

Jesus! I need you!

chapter ten

TUNNELS OF THE UNWANTED

Phena couldn't see anything. Not even the girl who was supposedly leading her into the underground colony of the orphans of Rome.

But she was no stranger to having faith, and so she relied on it as she continued to crawl through the dark and grimy tunnel. Her knees were throbbing, and her throat felt like it was closing in. It seemed like it had been hours of crawling already, but in reality, it had just been a few minutes. Out of nowhere, a sharp burst of light coming from the end of the tunnel caused her eyes to snap shut. Suddenly, her knees didn't hurt as much, and her lungs didn't feel so full of dirt. Then, the small, dirty, bare feet of the child ahead of her came into view.

Almost there.

Phena carefully climbed out of the tunnel, which opened into the room's ceiling, revealing a dimly lit square vaulted room with faded frescos painted all over the walls and cracked stone features of Minerva and Ceres. The walls were made of cement blocks, with six-foot breaks every ten inches or so. The breaks in the wall looked like they could hold a human body. *This is a crypt—a family crypt.*

The little girl who had guided her to the crypt immediately approached a taller, lankier girl, who couldn't have been more than twelve years old by her small frame,

but the look in her eyes betrayed an intimate knowledge of the world. Dirt and grime lined the creases of her olive skin. Her chestnut hair flowed freely down her back. She wore only a simple brown wool sack and no shoes. She sat on top of a simple stone-carved tomb that featured a relief of a boat that appeared to be sailing through a storm. The boat had let out its anchor, which was glowing in the water. *Is that a Christian grave?* The two girls were whispering, periodically glancing at Phena, who was still at the opposite end of the room, looking around.

"You! Hey!! Stay where you are!" The older girl yelled from across the room. Phena froze in her squatting position. "Why are you here?"

"Me? Are you talking to me?" Phena asked, immediately knowing how stupid she sounded.

"Yeah, who else?!"

"Right, ok. I'm Phena."

"Ok...? And?" The little girl in front of her groaned.

"And I just wanted to see-"

"See what? The sad existence of Rome's unwanted?"

"No, that's not what I was thinking..."

"Well, you've seen it. Now go!" The young girl that she had crawled through the tunnel with was about to return to Phena's side, presumably to escort her out of the orphan's carefully carved passageway.

"No, wait! Listen, I want to help. I know that-"

"What do you know? Huh?"

"I am an orphan, too. I want to help you."

Her companion piped in. "Maybe we should listen to her."

"Yes, thank you-?"

"My name's Sabina." Phena rose from her squatting position. "Sabina, if you want to know, I recently had my house burn to a crisp, and with it, my livelihood and my calling."

"So? You're poor just like us..."

"Yes, but-"

"She's wasting our time! Get her out of here!"

"Wait, I am determined to find myself a benefactor who will help me to start a home for orphans in the city. I would like all of you to join me there."

"You mean like a *Domus Pupillorum*?"

"Yes"

"An actual home?" Phena smiled, amazed that the concept was so astonishing to this curious little girl.

"Listen, Sabina, don't go dreaming with this crazy lady."

"But, Daria, dreams are all I have." Daria sunk back in her chair and made a gesture with her hands to continue.

"Sabina," Phena continued, "I plan to make a home for each of you!"
"Why would you do that?"

"I am a follower of the Way."

"Ugh!" the older girl dramatically scoffed as she turned around, seemingly done with Phena. "Listen, My Saviour and Master, call me to love others and care for the poor, especially the orphans. So that is what I want to do."

"Your Master cares about orphans?" Sabina asked, sounding slightly interested.

"Yes! Deeply!"

"That sounds nice..." She replied dreamily.

Phena knelt to look into the little girl's dark brown eyes. "I promise you that if all of this works out, you'll have a home!" The little girl's eyes immediately welled up with tears at the mention of the word 'home.' Phena could feel her entire body fill up with immense love for her and an intense desire to fulfill the commitment that she just made to her. *Thank you, Jesus, for this precious girl.*

"Ok, so what are you waiting for then?" Daria asked, still annoyed.

"Ok. I'm going. Next time you see me, I'll have news! I promise!"

"Do you need some help getting to the surface?" Sabina called out from behind as Phena began to climb back into the roofed tunnels.

"No, thanks. I know my way."

chapter eleven
ETIAM DOMINE

"This is it," Phosa whispered to herself, her hands cold and shaking. *I'm going to die. I'm actually gonna die!* She was surrounded by invading strangers and knew that this was the end. She would be found and traded as a prostitute or worse. She knew that resistance was futile, for she was at the mercy of these ruthless outsiders and their cruel intentions. All at once, she came to grips with her uncertain and terrifying end.

Phosa couldn't sit there hiding any longer. *Let's get this over with.* She stood up and marched towards her hovel, all the while looking behind her to ensure that the other two men did not see her. With the coast clear, she approached slowly. The man who had been knocking on their door had long since entered but had not come out yet. *He's waiting in there for me! God, give me strength.* She found a *sarculum*, hidden in some long grass and kept it close to her. She felt courage well up inside of her, knowing she had a way of defending herself. She slowly and quietly approached the shack. The wooden door let out a familiar creak as it swung open. Inside, her belongings were scattered throughout their humble one-room dwelling. She entered cautiously, relieved to find no one else there. Suddenly, a strong arm wrapped around her neck and a hand clamped tightly.

The muscles in her body instinctively tightened up as she struggled to free herself from the man's grasp. Then she remembered the weapon that had given her a sense of security only moments ago, with one great swing of her arm, struck her assailant as hard as she could. The man immediately released her and let out a wild yelp. Slumped over, the man agonized and then raised his now blackened eyes to meet hers.

"Why'd you do that?" His deep-toned voice grumbled, with his hand shielding his left eye.

"Who are you? What are you doing here?" Still wielding her weapon as she asked.

"I'm Decimus. You summoned me!"

"Decimus? Junia's servant?"

"Yes? Are you expecting another company to be in this *horreum?*" Phosa let out a deep breath and immediately felt the pressure in her head subside. "No, no, of course not. I'm really sorry for hitting you over the head."

"Apology accepted. Now, why am I here?" Phosa was relieved of the necessity of answering as Phena roughly tumbled through the door, leaving behind a cloud of dust and grime. Her tunic was stained with what looked like mud, and her face was caked with dirt.

"Oh! It's you!" Phena squealed excitedly, her arms wrapped tightly around Decimus' neck and her head buried in his shoulder as she squeezed him in a strong embrace. Phosa hadn't seen her sister this excited in a while and couldn't help but be confused. *How does she know him? I don't know him!* For the first time since he'd arrived, Phosa noticed how incredibly handsome their visitor was. His short brown hair, slightly tousled, framed a face marked by gentle strength.

His kind blue eyes, like the calm of a clear sky, radiated warmth. After a prolonged embrace, Phena released him.

"Were you in any danger coming?" Phena's eyes revealed her sincere worry.

"We are always in danger, you know this. But enough about me. I've brought you girls some provisions, but Junia tells me you asked for me specifically." His eyes danced with charm, that made even Phena blush.

"Yes, how is Junia? We haven't heard from her since the—-the night we —uh." Phosa still couldn't bring herself to discuss the night the fire broke out.

"She is well. You know Lady Junia. She keeps going no matter what the Romans do to her." *What does he mean by that?* Phosa wondered.

"I remember on that horrible night, one minute she was with us and the next she had disappeared." Phena paused, deviating her glance to the doorway. "We didn't know if she was saved or not."

"I'm sorry to both of you. You must know it is very difficult for her to get any word out here, and she took great risk allowing me to come here at all. For now, all you need to know is that she is safe."

"Yes we are very grateful." Phena lightly brushed her tear-dampened face, and suddenly, her face returned to her usual expression of determination. "There is much to discuss." Phena gestured her guest to sit on the chair behind him. "I have received word from God that we are to open a *Domus Pupillorum* for all of the orphans living outside of the city gates." *What? How could she not mention this to me?*

"Are you serious?" Decimus inquired, his tone reaching a higher octave.

Phena continued, paying no attention to his obvious puzzlement. "We would of course need help with securing the funds for such a venture."

"Well, you would need more than help. You would need a benefactor to act as your guarantor. But your father is dead?"

"Yes, he died not very long ago," Phosa piped in.

"And you don't have any brothers?"

"No brothers I'm afraid," Phosa answered again, her sister's stern glance warning her not to again.

"And no suitors"

"Ha!" Phosa laughed out loud, "No! Decimus, we are homeless, destitute orphans living off of the generosity of your Lady. We don't have any suitors."

Decimus only nodded. "So, you wouldn't be contributing anything to this project?"

"Not anything monetary, if that's what you're asking."

"Ok. First, let me just say, I am so encouraged by the work that you and your sister have put into the church network in Rome. As a follower, I am so thankful. And I am amazed that even after such a tragedy has befallen you that you are willing to start a brand new extensive work for the Lord."

"Thank you. That means a lot."

"That being said, what you are proposing is almost completely impossible for a patrician woman, let alone a plebian such as yourself."

"Oh.."

"Did your father not give you lessons in Roman law?"

"Uh, no, certainly not. Why would he need to?"

"Hmm, well, Roman law dictates that women cannot be engaged in business of any kind in their own right and may only exert that sort of influence under the authority of a male legal guardian, usually a father, brother, or husband. And I'm assuming you have none of those."

"That is true."

"Then, your only recourse is to find a wealthy man who believes in your cause and might be willing to execute this venture on your behalf."

"On my behalf?"

"Yes, that's the only way, and I know someone who might be able to help."

"I knew you would!"

"Wait, Phena, is this what you want? And, you might have forgotten that we don't exactly have a convincing plan or a home for that matter."

"I haven't forgotten sister. Decimus, please go on."

"His name is Sebius and he is a Jewish Moneylender on Via Vagus."

"Wanderer's Way?"

"That's the one."

"And you think he'll help?"

"He might, but you must pitch your proposal to him directly."

"How will we get into the city unseen?"

"That I cannot help you with. I took the same risk just coming to see you."

"OK. We will manage. We have to. Does Sebius take clients previously unknown to him?"

"Not usually, but for a sister, he will. I will send him a message so that he knows you are coming. And I'll ask Junia to send a cart for the personal items you may have. It might be imprudent to show up at this stranger's home with a cart full."

"Ok."

All this sounds too risky to me.... Phosa's words remained unspoken. She knew her sister's ears were completely closed to any questions.

"And Phena? Don't go at night. Or even in the evening. The streets are full of dark-minded men who have evil desires."

Etiam Domine

chapter twelve
NOW OR NEVER

The silent road in front of their shack awoke with the tumbling sound of rickety old wheels forcing themselves through the track marks. Decimus was as good as his word, sending them a cart in the dark of night. But it wouldn't be bringing them into the city; that was too dangerous.

"Phosa, do you have everything? The cart is here."

"Good, we'll have to be quick. We can't risk anyone seeing us."

"Where would the cart bring our things? Isn't it imprudent to just send a bunch of stuff to the Moneylender that we don't know?"

"Yes, that's why Decimus is arranging that we send our things to Junia's house first."

"But her house is under watch, isn't it?"

"Yes, but it's just a cart. And we have no other option."

The cart came and went with all their things. Now, they had no choice but to venture into the city that had so craved their blood. Phosa couldn't breathe. A hand was pushing down on her mouth, seriously restricting her air intake. Her body instinctively started to panic. Her entire body fought against this rage. Her mouth let out frantic moans. Phosa opened her eyes, expecting to see a rough, muscular assailant. Instead, she saw the soft features of her older sister. "Shhh, quiet! There are two men outside." Phosa nodded with her eyes, and the pressure on her mouth was released. She gasped for air.

"Sister, do you want to stop my heart?"

"You exaggerate!"

"NO, I-!"

"Shh-listen! Can you hear them?"

"No."

"Neither can I. They're on the move!" she angrily retorted, then got up slowly from their bed on the floor.

"Where are you going?"

"There are strange men on our land. I have to know what they're doing..."

"Sister, just come back. They're investors. They won't bother us if we are quiet"

"How do you know?" Phena asked as she cautiously looked out the window towards the well.

"I saw them the other day..."

"What? You didn't think to tell me?"

"Well, no," Phosa replied, now unsure of herself. *I probably should have told her. But there wasn't that much to tell.*

"Who are they? What are they doing?"

"Like I said, the well-dressed man is likely an investor, and the other is likely a builder."

"Junia must be warned. This is her family's villa." *True, but what is she going to do about it, sister?* "I heard them say that it wasn't abandoned."

"Well, if it wasn't abandoned, then what-?" Phosa asked, not really wanting to know the answer.

"The Romans must have forced her family from the house." The idea alone caused Phosa's stomach to turn inside out. Phosa imagined a unit of Roman soldiers marching out of town towards the grand villa and one of Junia's relatives waiting for their demise from the open atrium. The sound of metal clanging and heavy boots pounding the earth. The end.

"Oh God, Junia! Why didn't you tell us this?" Phena asked rhetorically as if she had the same terrible image in her mind.

"Maybe she's ashamed. Maybe she was there when they arrested her family."

"Don't pretend you know what happened." Phena's abrasive voice betrayed her worry.

"Sister, we've been given a way out. We don't need to be concerned about this any longer."

"They'll explore the grounds, Phosa! Any clever investor would. We have to go. Now." Both women frantically packed what remaining belongings they had into their sacks. Phosa was careful to bring her treasured green fabric, along with her stylus set and a pile of parchment. She handed a neatly folded pile of red cloth to her sister, "Here, don't forget this!" Phena only grinned and slid it into her bag. Phosa looked around the shack that they'd lived in for the last month, sure she wouldn't miss it.

She quickly snatched up the four copies of Paul's letter that she had been working on and stuffed them into her bag.

The bright sun had now given way to dusk. They didn't dare turn on any lights, knowing their unwanted guests were still lurking outside.
Phosa bravely peered out their window towards the villa. She was looking for the dim glow of a torch either inside or outside the house. Through the open windows of the house, She spotted a distant flame floating from room to room.

"They're still there. How are we going to go unnoticed?"

"Hoods up. Mouths shut!"

Phosa did as she was told and quietly followed her sister out the door. The night air was thick with strain and fear as Phosa and Phena made their way cautiously towards the road leading into the city. Phosa couldn't resist looking over her shoulder towards Junia's family villa. The dim glow of the torches flickered ominously in the windows, casting long shadows on the ground. Phosa's heart raced with each step, her mind filled with images of Roman soldiers tearing apart the home of their dear friend.

The sisters quickened their pace, the urgency of their escape weighing heavy on their hearts. The darkness of the night enveloped them like a shroud as they stepped onto the road. They had evaded one danger, but the city of Rome lay as a trap before them. As the Tiburtina Gate glared imposingly at them, Phosa had a very bad feeling about what they were about to do.

"Phena!" She whispered her sister's name into the night

"Shh, what?"

"Didn't Decimus tell us not to travel at night or even in the evening?"

"What choice do we have? Those men would have found us, and then we would be sent to the lions for sure!" *Surely not; women aren't just fed to the lions for being poor!*

"Come on, Phena! That's crazy. Maybe we'd be taken as slaves-" Suddenly, Phena turned on her heel and faced her with a fiercely determined look on her face. "Lions, Phosa! You have Paul's letters with you, don't you?" *Oh, by Juno, I do!*

"They would have paraded us naked through the streets of Rome as a price for Nero. Never forget how dangerous it is to be a follower."

There was nothing left to say and only one thing to do. Go through the gate and into the city. With both of their hoods securely draped over their faces, the sisters slipped into the city without so much as a word or glance from any soldier. The gatehouse and the streets were both vacant but for wandering stray dogs and the occasional cat. Phena started to increase her pace. She seemed to have a destination in mind.

"We're looking for a Wanderer's Way. It's just west of the center on this side of the Tiber."

"Wanderer's Way indeed."

"It's going to be a long walk."

As the girls drew closer to the center, the traffic on the roads picked up, as did the disturbing sounds coming from brothels and the numerous bars. Each open bar they passed revealed more unsavory characters, some over drunk, some enraged, and some lusty. The Via Tiburtina was a long busy drag, on a slight downhill slant, the cobble stone sidewalks were cracked and didn't drain properly, making her feet suffer from the cold and damp of the early morning. She made the mistake of paying too much attention to her feet and not watching where she was walking. As a result, she stumbled headlong into a middle-aged plebeian dressed in what smelled like a urine-soaked olive-colored tunic. His short black hair was drenched in sweat, and his drooping eyes betrayed his ill intent towards her.

"Ahh," His stinging gaze urged her to increase her pace. "What a fine piece of meat strolling out so late at night!" He made an attempt to reach out and grab her cape but narrowly missed.

"Phosa, RUN!" Phena yelled at her from a few paces ahead. Phosa thrust her body forward, concentrating on her feet and pounding the sidewalk as she fought to catch up to her sister. Phosa ran as fast as she could, dodging ox carts, pausing in the middle of intersections, and prostitutes gathered outside brothels. Her heart danced within her chest, and her throat felt like it would burn up. Knowing that the man who had threatened her was a distant concern, she hunched over and took a breath.

"Sister! The Tiber!" Phena yelled from a block ahead of her. The river was near. She knew it by the smell of sewage that assaulted her senses. Their destination was over the bridge and into *Trans Tiberium*.

As she stood with her sister on the *Pons Aemilius* and looked down into the rushing Tiber, it felt like they had cross into a different world.

The hectic nature of the city was behind them, and before them were sleeping villas, towering insulae, and small domus of the regular plebeian people. As the sun was rising, they arrived at the XIV district known as Trans Tiberium, where they would find Wanderer's Way.

"We're close now, sister."

Bustling markets began to open, slaves hurried about their errands, and the scent of freshly baked bread wafted through the air. Phena led the way with a quiet determination. Phosa could tell that behind her sister's calm demeanor was a worry that never left her. She watched as her sister scanned their surroundings, and Phosa did the same. They were back in the city, and even though their insulae had been in a completely different district, Phosa couldn't help but think about their friend and servant as he lay in the middle of that courtyard. Lifeless. She hoped beyond all hope that he had somehow survived and that one day, they would be reunited. She scanned the faces in the crowd, hoping to see his kind smile and hear his witty jokes once again. She appreciated how he never tried to convert them to his beliefs and had relied on that understanding for many years. *God forgive us!*

With each step, Phena's grip on Phosa's arm remained firm. Her fingers were strong and unyielding, a reassuring presence in the chaotic setting. Phosa couldn't shake the feeling of being watched, a prickling sensation that made her skin crawl. She clutched her bag tightly, the weight of their precarious situation settling heavily on her shoulders.As they turned into Wanderer's Way, the atmosphere shifted. The narrow alley was quiet and deserted, a stark contrast to the bustling main roads they had just traversed. Phena quickened her pace, her steps echoing in the empty corridor. Phosa followed closely behind.

Sebius's house looked the same as every other villa on the Wanderer's Way. Both sisters were pleasantly surprised at the sight of their hoped-for benefactor's house. Decimus had made it sound like she lived in the poor quarter, but that was not the case. The villa was at least two stories high and covered one city block. The sisters stepped off of the sidewalk to get their bearings. In the center of the city block was a large stone archway, big enough that a cart or litter could squeeze through it. About two meters into the archway, they could see a massive and beautifully decorated dark green metal door with a chestnut lion's head knocker in the middle of each door. To the right of the house's main entrance, there were four open-air market stalls selling various wares and services to the public. None of them were money lenders, so the sisters walked toward the left side of the house. This site had one very large market stall with the sign generator hanging over the sidewalk.

"This is it!" Phena declared, turning to her sister, who was still looking around as if someone was watching them. "Phosa, it's fine. We're here. Stop looking around like that. You're making me nervous. "I'm just doing what you told me to!"

"Shh, ok. The door's open. Let's go in."

Then, remembering something, Phosa reached out to stop her sister. "Wait!" She pulled out the long green linen that she'd placed in her bag and gestured for her sister to retrieve her blue cloth. "We should wrap these around us like a toga."

"Why would we do that?"

"Look at this place, sister!" Phosa yelled frustratedly, "We need to appear less common. It will only help our cause." Phena nodded, giving her reluctant approval. Phosa wrapped her emerald-colored linen around her hips and then her shoulders, hiding the dirt and grim on her overused tunic. Phena did the same with her cobalt-colored garment. *Ok, now let's go.*

Phosa walked in behind her sister. After navigating through the bustling streets of Rome, the silence of the shop was unsettling.

Just inside the doorway was a large wooden desk with some wax tablets stacked neatly, one on top of the other. But there was no indication that anyone had heard their entry, so Phena took the opportunity to look at the richly decorated space. The ceilings were higher than an average stall, with decorated carvings etched into the plaster.

There were dazzling frescos of the pagan god Mercury blessing the moneylender's business and on another wall, Lady Justice ensured that business is carried out fairly. Phena had never seen such beautifully colored frescos before.

"Have you ever seen anything so..."

"Beautiful?" Phena uncharacteristically squealed at the indication that someone was watching her. She turned and saw a young man, probably around thirty-five, with short brown hair and a tanned face with thin brown hairs speckled all over his face, as if he had just been shaving and hadn't quite finished. His eyes were a deep greenish-yellow, and his smile was genuine and amused.

Suddenly, there was a sound of something precious smashing into a thousand pieces. Phena and the young man both turned in the direction of the noise and saw Phosa standing closer to the door trying to steady an iron stand that a vose was standing on and was now disintegrated.

"So...so sorry." Phosa said, shuddering as she gazed obviously at the handsome shopkeeper.

"Uh, don't worry about it. My father will just get another one..."

"You're father's the money lender?"

"Yes, do you have an appointment with him?" The young man walked towards the desk at the entryway and started to look through the pile of wax tablets. "What's your name?"

"No...I...We don't have an appointment."

"Well, I'm afraid my father is booked up for months. All I can do is write you in."

"Yes, please," Phosa said, shoving her sister aside. "Could you handle our appointment by any chance?"

"Phosa!"

"What? I just..."

"No, no, my father handles all appointments. I'm just the shopboy."*A dangerously attractive and clearly rich shopboy.* Phosa thought to herself.

"Ok, anyway." Phena stepped forward again and pushed Phosa to the side. "We are in urgent need of your father's services. We were sent here by Decimus."

"Decimus? Do you mean, Decimus of Vicus Cyprius?"

"Yes."

"Are you a follower?"

"Yes."

"Of the Way?"

"Yes! Yes. And we need to speak with your father." *Phena! How can you be so rude to this incredibly handsome....* In a moment, Phosa couldn't control herself. She pulled Phena backward by her dress strap and forced her face close to hers. She could see in Phena's eyes that she wasn't ready to be handled thus and was only getting angrier.

"What is your problem? Her sister whispered angrily.

"What's *my* problem? You're being rude to the son of the man who is going to get us out of this mess." Phosa had meant to whisper but knew she hadn't by the look on the bewildered shopkeeper's face. Phena turned to look at him and then turned back to Phosa with an embarrassed look on her face.

"You're right."

Ok, let me do the talking... Without getting any further permission, Phosa stepped up to the gorgeous man. "What do they call you?" *God! I can't even ask a simple question without sounding stupid.*

"I'm called Simon. And what are your names?"

"I'm Phosa, and this is my sister Phena." Phosa could feel her lips quivering as she spoke. Every part of her body was completely aware of his gaze.

"Do we have to go into this now?" Phena asked in a loud whisper.

"If you would, that would help me explain things to my father..."

"I'll proceed then. We were hosting a house church and were warned that the persecutions in Rome were only getting worse. That night, our apartment complex was burned. We escaped the fire and then had to run from an angry mob that accused us of starting the fire."

"Wow, that's quite a story. Where'd you go? Another house church?"

"No, no, but that would have been a good idea." Why didn't Phena think of that? "No, we hid outside the gates of Rome."

"Until we could not hide any longer. You see, I feel that God has given us a particular task." Phena interrupted.

"We all have tasks."

"Yes, I believe that God wants me to start a *Domus Pupillorum*"

"Oh, what a novel idea." The young man said, weaving his muscular fingers through his curly hair. "It's a lot of work. And it takes a lot of money. You want my father to finance it?"

"Yes."

"Simon!" A confident elderly voice touted from deeper within the stall. "Have you finished writing the endorsements for Publius Aelius Stolo? He's in my atrium. I need it now!"

"I'm with clients, father!"

"Clients? Simon! We've talked about this!" The raging voice of a middle-aged man came roaring from the back of the shop and was drawing closer. The young man looked at them, clearly anxious. "You make the appointments; I make the deals."

"You better go.." He said apologetically.

"Go? Where? We told you we're homeless!" Phena asked as Simon gently pushed them towards the door.

"Well, sorry, I...."

"Simon!" Phosa's voice echoed through the air as the wooden door slammed into her face.

chapter thirteen

DISMISSED

Simon's words hung in the air, sharp and pointed like thorns, making Phosa feel completely humiliated and utterly confused. Didn't Decimus send word that we were coming? Why were we dismissed like unwanted bleating sheep? And what are we supposed to do now? She looked around at the empty back street they were on.

The street was lined with small wooden doorways, some leading to opulence and luxury and others to one-room shacks. Rich and poor were mixed in the city of Rome. The doorposts of the rich were easy to pick out; they were decorated with colorful flowers and banners, the noble family colors were proudly displayed, and even a few guards were standing at the ready, watching the streets for their masters. Phosa's mind raced with thoughts as she pondered their next move. She could see from the look on her sister's face that she was doing the same thing. They were visibly flustered by their abrupt dismissal. Homeless, hunted, and rejected, they were truly alone in a city that offered no solace. The sudden noise of laughter jolted Phosa out of her thoughts. A young boy ran past them, chasing after a stray cat that darted into an alleyway.

"We can't stay here," Phena finally spoke, her voice laced with determination. "

"Why did he do that?"

"He must have a good reason. His father didn't sound very happy."

"Well, he still shouldn't have done that." Phosa could hardly believe they were back where they started. On the streets.

"There's no point in being upset about it. We have to figure out what to do now."

"There's nowhere to go, Phena! Nothing to do!"

"Keep your voice down!" Phena rushed at her and placed her palm against Phosa's mouth like she was still a child.

"Get off of me!" Phosa tried hard to wiggle out of her sister's grasp. She pushed her hand away from her face, only to have it return. "I'm serious; get off!" Not knowing what else to do, Phosa bit her sister.

"Oww!" Phena's hand immediately retreated from her face as her sister bent over in pain. "You bit me!"

"You deserved it!"

"Oh, just come on!" Phena turned on her heel and started walking up the street. Phosa was sick of talking, so it was just as well. It was clear the moneylender wasn't going to do anything for them. Maybe there was a house church leader that would take them in.

"Sister, where does Junia live?"

"The far east end of the city, why?"

"Have you been there before?"

"No, but don't you remember we can't go there! The authorities know about her house church."

"Sure, but there has to be a way. Maybe Festus is still seeing clients."

"Really? Do you think we look like clients?" Phena asked, gesturing at the sweat and dirt stains on their *stolli*.

"We have to try something. Can we just buy some new pellas?" Even as she was saying those words, Phosa thought of the beautiful material she'd taken from the villa.

"Oh, you have lost it, haven't you? Do you think we have money?"

"Well, we might have something to sell."

Phosa, we are wanted criminals on the run from the *vigiles*. And women at that! We cannot take the risk of selling anything."

"Uh, ladies?" Phosa felt a delightful tingle from the bottom of her spine up to the nape of her neck. It sounded just like the young man she'd only just been cursing under her breath.

"Yes?"

"My father will see you now."

"He will?"

"Yes, we have just been talking and I think he might be persuaded to help you." Phosa thought she saw his eyes glide up to hers and land there for a few seconds in a familiar gaze. *Is he ogling me? No, that's not possible.* But even the thought of it made her cheeks flush.

Phena took charge of the awkward silence. "Ok, well, by all means, lead the way."

Simon led the women through the money lender's stall and into the back room that had two side doors, one leading to the stables and one to the main house. In the anteroom, there were two lounging couches and a tray of cheeses, grapes, and sweet bread.

"Please, enjoy some refreshments while you wait. I'm sure you're starving."

"Yes, thank you."

"I'll take my leave now."

"You're not staying with us?"

"Phosa!"

"No, It is my shift in the stall. But I will likely see you later on. There's a house church meeting here tonight." *I'll be counting the minutes.* Phosa shook her head, willing the thought from her mind. *Wasn't I just cursing him for leaving us out on the street? And now I'm gawking at him? Come on Phosa!*

"OK, sure. We will probably go, right Phena?" She answered maturely.

"Yes, we'll be there. Thank you, Simon." Simon smiled and nodded at his guests and then returned to the market stall.

"Phosa! You are so obvious; it's humiliating."

"What? What do you mean?"

"I mean, you're falling all over yourself."

"Well, have you seen him?"

"Yes, but we are here for business."

"Maybe you are…"

"What are you here for? A fixing?"

"A fixing? No! If I wasn't a Christian…then maybe…"

"Maybe what? He's way out of your league anyway! He's rich, and we're homeless. You need to just forget him." *Forget him? He's the only happy distraction I've had in months. I need something positive! Something trivial!*

The gorgeous features of that stranger had lifted her out of her homeless, destitute misery for a while- and what was the problem with that? The silence in the room was so thick it could have strangled her. But her sister didn't seem to mind or care. She just started the next task at hand: first, berate me until I want to cry, next eat something from the cheese tray. Phena's cold, calculating manner was starting to get to her. She wanted to see her sister fail, drop something, pour something down the front of her dress. She wanted to see her slip, and not just with her words. But then guilt slithered into her heart, like an unwanted vermin eating away fresh produce. She wanted to harbor negative feelings towards her sister, but she knew she shouldn't.

The two sisters sat in the moneylender's anteroom in complete silence for what felt like years. The room was very comfortable and spacious, with high ceilings and large windows that let in warm sunlight. It was furnished with luxurious rugs, two sofas with intricately embroidered cushions died in orange, and a large serving table in the middle. At the opposite end of the room was the studious writing desk, presumably where most of the master's business was conducted. Neat stacks of paper, piles of books, and two bottles of ink. The walls were painted red, but one large fresco of a middle-aged man with a beard, holding the hands of two small children as they walk down a lane into a large stone fortress. Curious. As the sisters sat down, two servants came with a tray of meats, cheeses, and bread, along with two goblets of wine. One servant quickly left, and the other stayed behind to light hanging gas lamps scattered throughout the room.

"Ladies!" said the kind voice of a middle-aged man as he entered the tablinum where they'd been waiting. "Sorry to keep you waiting." The man who stood before me, likely Simon's father, was of a tall stature and had a head of black hair sprinkled with patches of grey. His penetrating eyes were a deep shade of brown, adding to his intense presence. He wore a long silk tunic died in luxurious red and embroidered with gold threads. Despite his age, he had a remarkably fit and toned physique. He was not at all what Phosa had expected from the sound of his gruff voice.

"I hope you are enjoying the refreshments! Especially the wine! It's delightful. It comes from my uncle's vineyards just east of Ostia. You know, just a few generations ago, his family were slaves taken from Israel in the time of Pompeii. You've heard of Pompeii, yes?" Both girls nodded their heads, happy to allow him to jabber on. "But now his family, and mine for that matter, are very well-endowed thanks to the land that was preoccupied by my grandfather's former master. You see, he was such a wonderful barber for his master that he was written into his will. Am I boring you? I do apologize."

"No, please, keep going," Phena said politely.

"I was mostly finished. The bottom line is that I'm rich now, or else I couldn't be a moneylender. Or a house church leader, for that matter." *I'm pretty sure there are plenty of house church leaders that are poor.* "You two were house church leaders, yes?"

"Yes, until our apartment block burnt down."

"Yes, my son was telling me about that. You are fortunate to be alive."

"Yes, by the grace of God."

"You have been through a lot indeed, and I am happy to help you until you find acceptable matches, of course. In the meantime, you have a place to stay here in the villa for as long as you need. I just need your solemn word that you were not followed."

"No, no sir, we weren't followed."

"You were attentive to your surroundings?"

"Yes."

"And you have no prior connections with the Jewish quarter?"

"No sir,"

"And who else knows you are here?"

"Decimus"

"Ah, yes. Anyone else?"

"Yes, Junia! She knows."

"Junia? I've heard of her. She leads a house church in the eastern quarter."

"Yes, her church has had to meet elsewhere since the raid."

"She was raided?"

"I'm sorry. Can we get back to our application for your moneylending services? You haven't spoken to us about that at all." Phena prodded, sounding slightly rude.

"Yes, well. I'm sorry, dear, but I don't lend money to women. Their cases often go to *iudicium,* and with no *advocatus* of your own, I'm afraid-"

"Why would we need to go to iudicium?"

"That's the very thing that I could not explain to a woman. And anyhow, your idea, as wonderful as it sounds, doesn't make any sense."

"What do you mean?"

"You can't own property as a woman, especially as a woman who is not a *patricia* or at least an *equestrice.* And even then, unless you are widowed, you really have no right to begin a business venture. Do you have a dowry, or did your father leave you an inheritance?"

"No on both accounts, sir."

"Then I'm afraid you can't do this on your own, and I can't take this risk upon myself. Not without some sort of reward, at least."

What does he mean by that?

"But Decimus said that a woman can own her own property."

"Yes, but only in the name of a male guardian, which you don't have."
"What about Gaius?" Phosa piped in, just remembering that their legal guardian was probably their uncle.

"Gaius?!" Phena shouted back, clearly annoyed at her sister's interjection. "He'll never support this cause, and with the apartment building burnt to a crisp, his wealth has been either severely crippled or at least momentarily depleted. He is of no use to me!" Phena pronounced harshly. Her face glazed over with hopeless frustration. *Just trying to help*, Phosa thought.

"Listen, my dear, the only recourse you have is to either allow me to become your either your adoptive father or your husband." Phosa watched as a delicate pink shade overwhelmed her sister's cheeks.

"Husband?"

"Yes, my dear. If that option delights you. I would like to get the measure of you before I engage in such a contract, you understand." Phosa looked carefully at Sebius' face, her eyes scanning every feature for any signs of deception. He had a strong jawline and brown eyes that seemed to hold a hint of kindness behind them.

"Of course," Phena replied stoically. Phosa couldn't help but be confused. The Phena she knew would have vehemently refused such an offer if she had received it even a few hours ago, but now she seems to be up for it. *What changed? Does she want this orphanage thing to work out so badly that she will consider marriage? And marriage to a stranger?*

"Phena, can I talk to you for a second?"

"Later, sister, we are in the middle of a discussion here. My apologies, sir, but did I understand that the other option was for you to adopt me?"

"Well, yes, in theory, I could adopt you as my daughter."

"That seems like the less complicated option of the two, is it not?"

"Yes, and no. If I were to adopt you, my immediate recourse, as your legal guardian, would be to find a suitable match for you. Depending on whom you marry, he might support you or demand that you desist from any economic or real estate interests.

And I would also be required to supply you with a reasonable dowry, which is quite the investment as you can imagine."

"Are you willing all the same?"

Sebius' attention drifted towards the window that was left ajar in his office. He narrowed his eyes as if focusing on a specific object outside. He took in a deep breath and let it out with a sigh. Phena's intense gaze showed just how much she was relying heavily on this man's verdict. He turned away from the window and sat down at his desk, avoiding the prodding gaze of the ladies before him.

"I...I..uh. young lady, I would have to take some time to think this through. You understand that you are asking quite a bit from me, and we have only just met."

"Oh, sir, I understand completely."

"Let me finish. There are personal, legal and financial matters at stake here and for a sound answer to be given, I will have to consult my lawyers, financiers, and of course my Lord."

"Will you not mention this also to your son?" And heir, Phosa, almost added.

"Phosa!" Phena interjected, obviously ashamed.

Sebius, once again, quieted them both with one wave of a hand. "Phosa," His tone was calm yet commanding. "I can see that you do not understand how large households like ours work. "My son does not make the decisions for this household." He breathed deeply and let out a deep sigh as if he was ready to be finished with this conversation.

"Ladies, I will require at least two months to review the plans for your ideas and to have the consultations that I require in order to make an informed decision." Phosa glanced at her sister's face, trying to judge if she was relieved or concerned by such a delay. As usual, she revealed little on her face, but her fidgeting hands told another story. *She's nervous.*

"Sir, I understand you require time and proper counsel. I am just wondering if there is any way that I can assist in ensuring...."

"You could agree to marry me now."

"Sir?"

"Phena, my dear." Sebius's expression changed from one of seriousness to gentle affection. "I care nothing for class or ethnic distinctions."

Really? Phosa thought to herself, not sure if she believed him.

"You are a beautiful, smart Christian woman. What more could I ask for in a wife? And you are young. You may yet bare me more children. My late wife she-" Sebius's eyes glistened with unshed tears as he stared off into the distance, his brows furrowed and his lips trembling with suppressed emotion. The air seemed to grow heavy with the scent of sadness and longing as if Sebius's emotions were tangible and filled the room.

"Yes, tell us about your late wife..." Phena pried gently.

Sebius's muscular chest rose and fell like a great rushing river. "She, uh, died giving birth to my daughter. She did not live either. Perhaps you can make up for my loss." Phosa watched the two figures intently as they spoke. Sebius towered over her small, slight sister, his face overcome by the sorrow of his past. While she felt sorry for the terrible loss he has had to bear, Phosa was more concerned about her sister. She knew that Phena loved to rescue others. If anything would draw her into marriage, his sorrow-filled story would.

"I, I do not know what to say, sir. I am truly saddened to hear of the grief you've had to carry over the years. But I will need some time to consider your proposal." Phosa checked her sister's face, wondering what she thought of all this.

"Yes, of course you will. It was not right of me to pressure you. You will have my formal answer in eight weeks. But in the meantime, you will be our guests." Phena only nodded in return and bowed slightly as if she was going to leave.

"Please allow one of my maids to escort you to your chambers. And please feel free to walk the grounds anywhere you wish. The hortus is particularly soothing for the soul." He smiled graciously at both of them as he waved one of his attendants into the room. "Now, if you'll excuse me, I have some business to attend to." Sebius offered a hand to Phena, who accepted the gesture with a shy smile. He delicately applied his lips to her hand and then let go. Phosa stood by and watched, feeling completely invisible. Her mind raced, trying to make sense of the situation she found herself in.

"*Deus tecum sit.*" Sebius' farewell hung in the air as he closed the door behind them. Phena's face reddened to a hue Phosa had never seen before.

They both turned, and there in the middle of the atrium was a tall young girl with striking blond hair stretching just past her shoulders tied back in a respectable braid and blue eyes the color of the sea. She wore a simple white tunic to her knees and a single bronze bangle on her arm. The girl's smile was warm and inviting, making Phosa feel a little more relaxed.

"My name is Sarah; I will be here to attend to your every wish. Please follow me. I will show you your rooms and the rest of the villa." Phosa followed quickly behind the servant, looking for another access to the moneylender's stall, where she knew Simon was still serving out his shift. But there was no secondary entrance. Instead, she focused her attention on the detailed frescos decorating each wall, the carved busts of men she presumed were Sebius' ancestors, which were displayed on expertly carved stone columns throughout the open areas of the villa. Sebius' home followed the standard plan of most well-to-do Romans with a respectable atrium at the front, leading to the hortus and covered hallways at the back, where most of the private rooms of the house were located. The gardens were expansive and beautifully appointed with stone walkways, elegant statues of Roman gods and goddesses, and one particularly interesting fountain featuring the vestial fires of Rome. *Ironic in so many ways,* Phosa thought to herself. At the opposite end of the garden was an elegant cushioned dining room, where they would likely take their meals. Turning back towards the covered corridor, Sarah showed them their small rooms.

"This one on the right is assigned to you, Phena. And the other is for you, Phosa." Phosa wasn't sure she liked the special treatment that her sister was obviously getting already. Her sister's room was much larger than hers and was appointed with luxurious silks, fine frescos, and even a colorful rug.

"I await your request, but I will leave you now to settle in." Phena smiled as they tested out the softness of her mattress.

"Thank you, Sarah." Phena politely dismissed her, still admiring the silk material of her sheets. Seeing the simplicity of her own room, she had no need to rush off and inspect it. She really wanted to know what had just happened in the anteroom with Sebius. Now's my chance. I have to say something.

"OK, sister, Talk. What was that all about? You seemed too willing to consider his proposals." Phosa's eyes searched her sister's face for answers. But only found resistance.

"Phosa, we are in a precarious situation. Our home is gone, our future uncertain. If there's a chance to secure our safety and possibly rebuild what we've lost, we must explore every avenue."

"But marriage? You have always said you would never marry! These are drastic measures, Phena, at least for you they are!" Phosa insisted, her worry for her sister palpable. She shrugged and did as she was told. "Sebius' offer, either of them, might be my only hope of starting this orphanage.

"So, you want this so much that you'll marry a stranger?"

"God has led us here. That is obvious to me. And Sebius seems like a good Christian man of means. Perhaps this is the Lord's will for me."
"Or you could let him adopt you."

"You heard what he said. That would come with extra complications that could derail my mission."

"Your mission? Your only hope? Phena, where do I stand in all your plans? You're my older sister! You're supposed to be looking out for me!" Phena's eyes softened a rare vulnerability showing through her normally composed demeanor.

"Phosa, my dear sister, you must understand. We serve a God who is good and who loves us. He has a plan for both of us, and He is in control. Take comfort in that! As for the orphans' house, I vow to you that I will not make any decisions that would harm or neglect you." Phosa felt a surge of conflicting emotions within her - admiration for her sister's unwavering faith and determination, worry for the uncertain road ahead, and a twinge of resentment at being left out of the decision-making process.

"But Phena, what about what I want? What about my dreams and hopes?"

"God knows them all. Rest in that."

Phosa retreated to the private room that Sebius had so graciously offered her, even if it was a far cry from the luxury that Phena was offered. It was a godsend to have a moment of peace and quiet away from the judgmental glances and wagging fingers of her older sister. Phosa lay down on the bed and looked up at the freshly painted yellow plaster ceiling. Even after seven weeks, it was difficult to get used to her rich surroundings. She'd never been in a room with painted ceilings before. The room was comfortable with fashionable wood furnishings, a heavy solid wood framed bed, and two wooden chests full of women's clothing exactly her size. She had to admit that Sebius had been very generous, but she suspected that it was because he was in love with Phena and not out of kindness. There was also a small sitting table with a mirror that had perfumes and cosmetics, most of which Phosa had never even seen before, much less used.

Phosa examined the beautifully painted scenes on the walls of Heracles overcoming his foes and then of Bacchus recovering a bounty of grapes from a luscious landscape. *Why would a Jew have such murals painted? Were they the works of the previous owners? Or did Sebius commision them? Was he trying to impress his guests? Does he have very many overnight guests to impress? Surely he and his household must be against the pagan religions?*

Phosa was genuinely curious and hoped they would talk about that later. Phosa's heart ached with the weight of her sister's words. She wanted to trust God and have the faith that her sister had, but as she stood there in her sister's coveted private chambers, the knowledge that her sister had likely found a husband before she made her want to claw those pretty green eyes out of her head.

chapter fourteen

WILL HE OR WON'T HE?

Still no answer.

At first she rested all her hopes on their brilliant and rather handsome benefactor, finding some sort of arrangement that would not only be feasible, but would bring them all what they wanted: for Sebius, a viable investment and for herself, a usefulness that completed her. But now, she was sure that she wanted more than that. She was sure that for the first time in her life, she wanted to be a wife. His wife.

At first, she spent her days wandering the villa, searching for something to occupy her time, which felt like a futile search without a proper role within the household.

She envied her sister's literary abilities, which made her role in the household more secure. She could read and write, so she was sent to work in the moneylender's stall. Each morning, Phena chuckled to herself as she watched her sister leave the house to start her shift in the stall. Her sister's smile revealed everything: she had a crush on the boy, Simon. Phena really couldn't blame her sister. He is the only boy in the household that would even be remotely appropriate for her. And he is a Christian.

Perhaps, if Sebius suddenly doesn't want to marry me, she can marry Simon. But just the thought of such a thing made her anxious. She didn't want the moneylender to reconsider. For the first time in her life, she was sure she did want to marry. Phena resolved herself to learning how to be a domina, even if she was not one yet. A difficult task since the servants wondered why they should listen to her, and she had no ready answer. *My determination will speak for itself soon enough. At least, I hope it will.*

Her resolve only grew after each banquet, receiving the adoring glances of her would-be lover, which turned into honored recognition in front of many from the patrician families of Rome. At first, it felt strange to stand next to a powerful and handsome man she barely knew and pretend to be a great lady, but soon, the familiar curl of his lips as he greeted his guests brought her comfort and then even a pang of desire. Night after night, standing by his side, she longed to stand even closer to him, to hear the reassuring gentleness of his commanding voice was, like healing balm for her soul. She no longer felt like an imposter, a cleaned-up dog wearing beautiful clothes. With Sebius' encouragement and doting, she started to believe what he was telling her. *I am his domina.*

As the weeks went on, she slipped into the role of mistress without even meaning to. She dictated many notes of thanks to Sebius' banquet guests, sent orders to manufacturing and warehousing firms, arranged for servants to attend market days, greeted clients in the atrium, monitored the brewing process in the outer buildings, and supervised the care of the animals in the stables. She was especially proud of her care of the hortus sanitatis, which had fallen into disuse. She noticed the servants' amused expressions when she herself bent down to rupture the rock-solid soil, dig it up, and make way for fresh plants. She didn't care that mistresses often did not do such things. The raw smell of the dirt and the fresh air brushing against the plants refreshed her soul.

"I can't tell you how beautiful you are right now." Phena gasped and ungracefully fell backward onto the stone path beside her work area and immediately felt embarrassed. She quickly stood up, brushed her dress off, and bowed her head in his direction out of respect, blushing as she did. A man like Sebius had never before called her beautiful.

"There's no need for that." He said, with an amused grin spread across his wide lips. For the first time, she noticed how kissable his lips looked. He reached out to help her up, and she gladly accepted his hand. But she was immediately caught off guard when he pulled her tightly against his muscular body, so close she could feel the beating of his heart and the warmth of his breath.

"Phena?" His eyes pierced hers, a look of raw longing so vulnerable she could hardly breathe.

"Yes?" She couldn't help but imagine all the things she wished he could do to her.

"I think, I uh." His hands gently caressed the small of her back as he closed his eyes and leaned in.

"Yes?" His eyes opened, and his lips grazed hers in an agonizingly slow, teasing manner. "I have to confess that I desperately want you."

"You do?" She asked, knowing how ludicrous the question was. His desire was glaringly obvious.

"Yes, God forgive me. I need to have you." His hand gently traced her side, gliding up and down the edges of her body. She could tell he was trying to be respectful and chaste but desperately did not want him to be.

As his hands moved, her feelings for him only grew stronger and more certain. His hands made their way to her face, gently caressing her neck, then cheeks and her plump lips; all the while his eyes never left hers.

"Sebius...I"

"Phena, you must marry me. You must, or I might go mad."

She saw in his eyes a wild look of need and desire that would be fulfilled if they kept this up. And she didn't have the strength or even the will to resist him taking her right there in the middle of his garden. The thought sent a warm sensation throughout her body. She looked around to see if anyone was watching.

"Sebius-"

"Phena, It is not just your beauty that draws me. I am but a simple man desperately enamored by a graceful, intelligent, hard-working woman. But I cannot lie. Your beauty has memorized me!" Sebius' words hung on his lips, the lips that had only moments before grazed hers.

"Sebius,I will marry you." In a moment, his eyes turned from a desperate longing to ecstatic joy. She barely finished speaking when he picked her up in the air and let out a shout of ebullience that she was sure even the baker down the street could hear. She laughed at him, his joy contagious, and let relief wash over her. And then, in a flood of ecstasy, Sebius pulled her close to him again and pressed his full lips onto hers. The taste of his lips was sweet and comforting. She gave in to the pleasure of the moment, pressing herself even tighter against him. Phena's hand instinctively reached up to tenderly stroke his cheek, relishing in the strength of his jawline and the softness of his skin. She ran her fingers through his hair, feeling each strand between her fingertips. *He is mine. And I am his.*

"You know you really shouldn't be stuffing your face like that." Phena said harshly, her appraising glare making judgments of her as she reached her graceful arm across the table to take from the assorted feast they had before them. As her sister reached over her, she noticed the strokes of freshly painted gold henna adorning her lower arm and then the flash of light reflecting off of a solid gold bracelet featuring delicate filigree patterns that twisted and curled like vines around the wrist. *That's new.*

"I'm hungry," Phosa replied as she shoved a second hard-boiled egg into her mouth. Next, I think I'll try those oysters. The platter was full of smoked cheeses, salted mackerel, duck stuffed with onions and herbs, and even stuffed dormice and a bowl of fresh fruit from across the Roman empire.

"Suite yourself, but you will regret it later, I assure you!"

This was the first time in weeks that they'd had dinner together or even really seen each other. Phosa had barely caught a glimpse of her sister since they'd arrived, and when did she? She was hanging off Sebius's arm. She had to admit her sister was cunning in her deceit, for surely, no matter what she said about it, Phena had no intention of marrying Sebius. But honestly, she didn't really care what Phena was up to.

She was too busy trying not to single-handedly sabotage Sebius's entire business. And it was all because of Simon. She had been tasked with the role of writing down every financial entry, keeping records of his client's transactions and repayment schedules, entries in the appointment book, and a dozen other tasks she felt far too unskilled to perform. But she could think of nothing but Simon: his breathtaking face, the sound of his sensual voice as he spoke about his love of the chariot races, and the charm of his teasing laughter.

A paralyzing yearning for him consumed her. His face haunted her dreams every night and seared into her mind with an intensity that left her breathless. Every shadow, every fleeting glance in sleep was filled with him, as if her very soul craved the sight of him, refusing to let go even in her unconsciousness. And it had all happened so quickly.

She often wondered if he knew. He must. Deep in her heart, she longed to confess her feelings to him. However, the words refused to leave her lips. She had no certainty of his feelings towards her and was afraid of rejection. But the last few days had given her a whisper of hope. Just that morning, she'd caught his eyes wandering as he spoke to her, lingering in ways that he shouldn't. Her whole body erupted in desire as she remembered the way his powerful hand felt as he held hers as they discussed their families, faith, and dreams. Phosa broke herself of her daydream, knowing them to be useless folly. Despite her strong desire for him to reciprocate her feelings, she understood that it was an unattainable dream.

"Phosa?" Her sister asked, clearly annoyed.

"Yes?"

"You've been ignoring me for like ten minutes straight."

"Oh, sorry. There's a lot on my mind."

"Is there? I would think there's only one thing on your mind." *You're a mind reader now, are you?*

"Well if you know so well, please tell, sister."

"Simon."

To her utter humiliation, Phosa's cheeks immediately flushed a delicate pink. "What of it?" She could hear how unconvincing she was.

"I knew it!" Phena laughed, "You're in love with him, aren't you?" Phosa was torn between confiding in her sister and pushing her away, so she remained silent.

"Well, I think you should look elsewhere."

"What? Why is that?" Because you want his father? Is that it? It was pretty obvious to anyone who had eyes that Sebius was interested in her sister. For weeks, she'd been watching her sister be strung along by their all-powerful benefactor. She'd seen them holding hands discretely as she laughed at his jokes and watched her expression as he bent over to whisper into her ear. And here she was, disparaging her feelings.

"Oh, there's just lots of men around."

"Really, name one...". But Phosa didn't mean it. She didn't want to be shown any other men. She just wanted Simon. They had chosen to take their dinner in the outdoor dining room, surrounded by lush greenery, with colorful flowers spilling over the edges of the table. Phosa was still enchanted by the serene sound of water trickling along the canals and waterways that lined the couches, spilling out into a beautiful fountain in the middle of the garden. It was quite a leap from their previous lodgings. Her appetite left her, and so did her desire to listen to another word. Phosa rose from the couch they were reclining on, and immediately, a servant came to retrieve her plate.
  As the sun began to set, its warm glow seeped into her room, creating a soft light that illuminated the mosaic floor tiles. It was almost time for the house church meeting.

Her thoughts returned to their last fateful meeting in what is now a burnt-up pile of rubble in the middle of the city. She'd never allowed herself to wonder if someone had set the fire on purpose. It's Rome. Fires happen every day. Surely, it was an accident. Then she thought of their trusted friend and servant, Rusticus. Lying there on the darkened stone of the open courtyard. He went into the fire for them. And paid for it with his life. Guilt and shame welled up inside of her and flowed out in a single tear. With all her heart, she wished she could go back and redo that night.

Phosa sat up and took in a deep breath of fresh air. *Ok, time to focus. Simon is going to be there tonight. I need to make up for my terrible first impression!* She rose from the bed and unlocked the heavy wooden chest. Inside, there were at least five different tunics, each one a different color and pattern - ranging from soft yellows to deep sky blues to vibrant pinks. All of them were made of the finest silk and decorated with various beads along the front, with a gold clasp attaching the straps to the back of the dress. She decided to wear the dazzling yellow flowing tunic, which featured one shoulder strap and a beautiful light blue stone-studded golden belt that accentuated her waist. Next, she ventured over to the makeup dresser and started to explore the cosmetic boxes, not feeling overly confident. Then she heard a knock on the door

"Yes?"

"Domina, Phosa. It is Sarah, your handmaid."

"Yes, come in."

Sarah gracefully moved into the small room, her simple white stola flowing in the wind as she walked, revealing a slim figure. "Thank you, Domina. Please, let me help you with the cosmetics." Her smile lit up the room, and Phosa came to appreciate Sarah's genuine desire to help her.

She guessed Sarah was about eighteen by her smooth, youthful face and bright, innocent brown eyes. The girl held up a small round container.

 "Shall we start with the rubrica? It will give your cheeks a youthful glow." She opened the container slightly to reveal a red powder.

"Yes, please do it with me as you see fit. If I can be honest with you....Sarah...?

"Yes, domina. I will speak to no others."

"I would like to draw the eye of a particular young man tonight."
"Oh, well, I really must do a good job then, domina." They both giggled as Sarah went about her work, applying charcoal to her eyelids, a red cream to her lips, and kohl to outline her eyes. After quite some time, Sarah's hands were empty. She simply bowed and left the room quietly. Phosa gazed into the reflection. The creature before her was a mature, beautiful woman. She hardly even recognized herself, and that was a good thing.

chapter fifteen
LIMITED PROSPECTS

Phosa's hands trembled in anticipation, her fingers fidgeting with the hem of her dress. Her lips tingled with excitement, her cheeks flushed. She couldn't stop glancing at the door as if Simon would come bounding into her room at any moment. Phosa paced back and forth in front of her mirror, admiring the way the fabric hugged her curves, and the light caught the intricate sapphire on her belt.

Phosa walked down the long hallway, her steps slow and deliberate. At the end of the corridor was an open courtyard shaped like a large square. Within the courtyard were three seating areas, each prepared for the guests who would arrive soon.

Servants were coming and going, bringing skins of wine, and trays of cheeses, grapes, and sweat meats. The room was richly decorated in lavender and rosemary petals and even more fountains were turned on. The walls of the corridor and inner rooms were skillfully covered with cream plaster; the edges of doorways were trimmed with silver edging. The mosaic floors had been polished since dinner time, and mimicked tiny schools of fish.

She could smell the intoxicating delights of the food set out around the room and felt her stomach grumble, even though she had already gorged herself on dinner a number of hours earlier. She scanned the area and noticed that, aside from the servants, no one else had arrived yet. Without caring much about etiquette, she rushed to claim a cushioned seat in the open-air dining room that she had occupied only hours before.

"Phosa!" She didn't have to turn around to know who was yelling at her.

"Phosa! You can't just claim the seat of honor! You must wait for the host!"

"Come now, sister! I'll just move when others arrive!" She answered unapologetically. *Honestly, you're such a....*

"Good evening, my ladies." As soon as Phosa heard his voice, shivers ran down her back. She hurriedly patted her dress flat and readjusted her reclining position on the couch.

"Good evening, uh, Simon." She managed.

"Enjoying yourself, I see?" Simon asked with a snicker.

"Yes, thank you. Your couch is very comfortable. And your decorator is quite skilled." Simon grinned, clearly very amused by the sisters. "Thank you!"

"Simon, your father mentioned there will be a surprise guest. Your father hasn't even told me of this mysterious visitor's identity. Will you be an *amicus* and spoil the surprise for me?" Phena asked.

"I'm afraid not. I've been put under strict orders not to tell anyone."

"Whyever for?"

"My father's amusement."

Oh, well, we must keep the moneylender amused!

Then Sebius entered the courtyard with three servants in tow. "Friends! Friends! I'm so sorry to have kept you waiting." Sebius spoke loudly, his voice echoing through the open garden. He stood in the center of the crowd, beckoning his servants to assist him with his crimson outer robe. They quickly attended to him and then retreated with his lifted garment.

"Please feel free to eat and drink during the course of the evening. I have a few announcements to bring to your attention: first, please welcome two new additions to my household: Tryphosa and Tryphena."

Phosa's face flushed with embarrassment as she suddenly realized that all eyes were fixed on her. Most looked on with friendly smiles and nods. While others just looked with curiosity.

"They have come to me with a new proposition for furthering the Kingdom of God and will be staying in my household until that plan comes to fruition. Another announcement, we are putting together a tithe for our brothers and sisters in Jerusalem who are experiencing hardship. Please pray about what you can or should give, and we will collect it at our next meeting. But now, without further ado, I would like to introduce you to my esteemed guest, Rufus. Rufus is the son of Simon of Cyrene, the very man who carried the cross for our Lord."

A heavy-set middle-aged man with long flowing brown robes and a grey beard came out from a room off of the courtyard. Phosa could see that his face was lined with age, his mouth slightly dark with thirst, and his eyes weary but joyful.

From his rough, angular features, dark and bushy eyebrows, and ample forehead,she could tell that he was not Jewish by birth. Phosa stood there and stared, frozen in time. The air was charged with a collective hush as if all the sound in the world had been sucked into a vacuum and replaced by awe and reverence for the esteemed guest among them. Even the garden birds seemed to still their song, as if they, too, were captivated by the presence of this man and his parentage. She wondered if Rufus himself had laid eyes on the Messiah. Or if he had watched their Saviour carry the cross to His place of judgment.

"Welcome, Rufus!"

"Hello, brothers and sisters. God Bless you! It is a great privilege to be here with you tonight. But I regret to inform you that I have not come with happy tidings. I have come with a warning of evil and hardship. And most of all, I have come to challenge you. Let's begin. As he said those words, the hands of several men and women slid up as if they had a question. "I'll take questions at the end if time allows it." The men and women nervously dropped their hands. "These are dangerous times. We do not know how long we will have, so I will get straight to the point. There is severe persecution coming to the church of Rome. And indeed, some of our brothers and sisters have already felt its fury."

As Rufus spoke, Phosa became so engrossed that she almost forgot Simon was standing next to her. A brief glance at him revealed that he, too, was lost in thought. A tall, dark servant passed by with a copper tray of glasses full of red wine. Simon pounced on the tray as if it contained eternal life, swinging down the contents of two goblets within seconds. Perplexed, Phosa returned her attention to Rufus.

I have had the privilege of sharing the gospel with members of the Senate." *There are Christians in the curia?*

"This brother has revealed to me that Emperor Nero is mad with rage for the Christians. He sees Jews and Christians as being part of one religion that is becoming a thorn in the side of the Empire. He saw how the expulsion of the Jews by his step-father Claudius did nothing and is coming up with a new, more severe plan."

"So what's his plan?" An unknown male voice asked.

"He means to enforce every citizen in Rome to register their household gods with the authorities. If you do not register any household gods, then you will be imprisoned."

"But, I thought Jews were exempt from the state religion!"

"Hey, we're not all Jews here!"

"Good point! But to answer your question: that was the policy of previous emperors. There is no evidence that Nero will uphold that policy." As Rufus spoke, worried whispers broke out among the crowd, drowning out his voice. "But listen, friends, we are not debating the likelihood of persecution. You, as Christians, should expect it every single day. What we are debating is how you will deal with it. You must know the parable of seeds. Jesus spoke of the different ways that seed is either accepted or not accepted in the soil." *What does seed have to do with anything?*
"Stay with me, I know. I have a point. The seed represents the gospel and how we receive it in our hearts. So, my friends, how have you received the gospel? Have you received it in faith during good times, but when persecution comes, will you deny it? Have you received it in good faith, but are you slowly letting the worries and fears of this world entrap you into forgetting who is in control? Or are you allowing the seed to take root, to the point that no matter what happens out there, he said, pointing towards the front door of the house, you will stay firmly rooted in Jesus? Take your time and think about this. Your eternal soul depends on it."

Phosa was both inspired and terrified by the parable. *What type of seed am I? How am I supposed to know? How do I be the right type? Oh, God! Help me!*   In a sudden movement, an older man rose from his seat. He appeared to be of Roman descent with his clean-shaven face and attire of white linen, specific to the fashion of ancient Rome. His face looked stern and ruffled by confusion.

"So what exactly are you asking us? And no more riddles!"

"I'm asking you if you are willing to die for Jesus. If you're not, then don't play at being one of his followers." The confusion on the man's face turned into a look of deep thought as he sat down. "Make sure you mean it." The older man retained a stoic glare as he slowly sat down in silence.

"Thank you, Rufus, we needed that." Sebius stepped forward and placed a hand on Rufus' shoulders in brotherly affection. Then he turned his glance to the house church members. "And Rufus is right. Persecution is coming and has been confirmed across several other house churches across the city. We may not have to be worried about showing our faces in public yet but mark my words; there will be a time. Control your fear. And remember the Way, the Truth, and the Life."

"Amen!"

"You are all dismissed. Please leave a few people at a time through the front door. My servants have advised me that there is no one on the streets at the moment, so your journey should be unhindered. Go in peace!" Sebius bowed shallowly towards his guests and then turned to speak with Rufus again.

"Well, that was intense." Simon casually stated, as if they were watching a horse race.

He stretched his arms and roughly grabbed a goblet of wine from a nearby servant's tray. His eyes looked dazed as they returned to focus on her. Phosa hadn't been around very many drunks in her life, but she could tell something was off with him.

"Simon, are you ok?"

"Oh, me? Little....old....me? Of course!" He let out a hysterical laugh that confirmed his condition. *Yep, drunk.*

"Hey, listen, Phosa, will you come with me?"

"What? Go with you where?" *Why would he even ask me that? Is he trying to disrespect me?* As if anticipating what she was thinking, he quickly retracted what he said.

"Oh no, no, no, no! That's not what I meant. I meant just for a walk to talk or....something."

Well, I suppose that sounds harmless. "All right. But where?" She looked around at the dozen or so people who were still crowded around his father's living room.

"Not here. Come with me." He gently grabbed her hand and led her, stumbling slightly, through the far opening of the courtyard that led out into a second open-air courtyard. She looked behind her for a moment, wondering if anyone saw what they were doing. She didn't want her reputation to be tarnished, especially since it seemed like they were Sebius' guests for a while. In a quick second, her eyes met her sisters, holding a wine goblet and standing next to Sebius with an air of dignity she had never seen in her. *Is she contemplating actually marrying him?* Already, she could see her sister had changed. Still being pulled along by her own love interest,

Phosa shifted her attention to the gorgeous, if drunk, boy in front of her. The distant chatter of the depleted crowd was behind them. And before them was a beautifully designed garden with stone walkways and arches covered in green vines, with flowers of every shape, size, and color jutting out to welcome the visitor.

"This place is beautiful!"

"Yes, it was my mother's. She designed the whole thing." *Maybe he's not drunk.*

"Were you very close?"

"Yes, I could tell her anything."

"I'm so sorry, Simon!" She gently touched his shoulder, just to make sure he knew that she meant it. To her surprise, he didn't push her hand away. Instead, he softly removed it from his shoulder and pressed his lips to the tips of her fingers, one by one. His gaze remained locked on hers the whole time. The moment sent fireworks up her back and an empty discomfort in her stomach. All at once, she was thrilled and terrified. *Does this mean anything? Or is he just playing with me?* A plethora of questions swirled in her head, but she forced herself to refocus on his eyes. She broke away from his hold and tried to regain her composure.

"So, tell me about something..." Something? Ughh! She didn't wish this often, but right then, he wished she could be more like her sister, who seemed to have the words for every scenario. *Think!*

"Something?" He laughed, his eyes playfully dancing. She suddenly grazed the tips of her fingers just to remember how his lips felt on her skin. "How about I do the asking since I brought you here."
That's fair "If you could ask for anything, absolutely anything, what would it be?"

As he asked, he shifted his body closer to hers until their shoulders brushed, the warmth of his presence enveloping her like a gentle embrace, and the soft glow of the flickering lanterns around them cast a dreamy light that made her heart race with anticipation.

She closed her eyes for an instant, trying to fight the urge to confess everything to him right then and there. She loved the way that he was looking at her and the soft warmth of his touch, but she knew it had to be meaningless. *He is a rich patrician, and I'm a homeless orphaned plebeian. Nothing is going to change that.*

Deciding she'd be half honest, she answered him, "I'd like to be married. Most of the girls my age are married already." She watched as his kissable lips formed into a charming smile as if she'd just said everything that he'd hoped she'd say.

"Phosa, I've really enjoyed our days together." He gently took her chin in his hand and turned her gaze upon him. He pressed her with his eyes, searching for something. She knew if he searched for too long, he would find it. Her passion for him was bare and vulnerable, naked for all to see.

"Phosa, Phosa. Sometimes, I just love saying your name." His powerful hands moved to caress the side of her face and delicately stroked her long brown hair, sending her into a frenzy of longing she was sure she couldn't resist. The soft words he breathed into her ear were irresistible to her. The realization of his sculpted body being so close to her was intoxicating. She knew that if she sat there with him for one more minute, she would succumb to his charms.

"Simon, I..."

"Yes, Phosa?" He didn't allow her to answer but took her face in his hands and kissed her full lips, revealing the longing and passion that he hadn't put to words yet.

She eagerly returned his ardor. Their kiss was filled with a fervor that consumed them both, igniting a fire within Phosa she had never experienced before. In that moment, all doubts and fears melted away as they stood there, lost in the intensity of their embrace, until she no longer knew nor cared where she was or who might be watching. Simon's passion only compounded, his hands cautiously gliding along her neck, down her back, and then across to her inner thigh. Feeling that that was enough, Phosa pulled away, her chest heaving with a mix of emotions—desire, confusion, and guilt all swirling inside her. She looked at Simon, his eyes dark with passion, and she knew that what had passed between them would change everything.

"Phosa, please tell me you have no suitors." He said with a glowing desire that she'd never noticed before. She laughed out loud, thinking about how ridiculous it would be if she did.

"Of course not!"

"I had to ask."

"Since you're asking, do you? Have any prospects?"

"Nope, no prospects. Completely free!" He grinned, pulling her to him again. "But...how could that possibly be? I mean, look at you. Did I just say that?" Simon just grinned sheepishly, as if he'd never heard anyone call him handsome before.

"Thanks, I think. But it's true."

"Oh, Simon, if you're asking for the reason, I think you are. We can't."

"What do you mean?"

"You know we're completely destitute. I'm plebeian. I have nothing to offer. I'm sorry, I have to go. It's late."

"I haven't offended you, have I?"

"No, no. It's just…It's late." She stood up from her seated position on a stone slab bench and turned her back to go back the way she came. "Phosa wait"! He firmly grasped her wrist and swung her back within an inch of his face. Part of her wanted to stay in this moment and see what he would say. But the more prudent side said it was a waste of time. Regardless, she couldn't resist his strong grip.

With his eyes searching hers and his soft hands grazing her right cheek, he whispered, "I will have you no matter who you are!" Simon leaned in, his lips so close to hers that she could feel their warmth on her. She was locked in that moment, as if time stood still, waiting to see what else he would do and how far he would go. Her mind and body were at war. She knew she should resist him, even just for her chastity, but her resolve was breaking under every tender glance. His lips finally met hers in an epic dance of longing and desire. In that moment, all her doubts and worries vanished.

chapter sixteen

A SIGHT FOR SORE EYES

Blurry rays of sunlight invaded Phosa's eyes, an unwelcome reminder that it was morning. Her vision still blurry, she stretched out, flipped her bare feet onto the floor, and tried to stand. Even the bowl of warm water placed before her could not provide any solace or comfort. She just wanted to return to the glorious dream where Simon's touch was not forbidden, and she…

"Phosa"! Her sister shouted from behind a closed door. Phosa! Aren't you up yet? Come on, you're late already!"

"Late? What for?" Phosa moaned.

"I'm just dressing. What's the rush?"

"Sebius has assigned you to help with the stall this morning."

"Me?" Phosa yelled back as she slipped into her freshly washed dress.

"Yes, you, oh, moaning genius! Best Scribe in all of Rome!"

"Uhgh, Phena! Would you knock that off!" Phosa shook her head, frustrated by her sister's sarcastic exaggerations. They were much more entertaining later in the morning.

"Who will be at the stall?" Phosa asked casually, imagining that after the evening's indulgences, Simon would have the morning off.

"You know who? Just get out here!" Then, she heard the tiptap of Phena's shoes echoing against the stone walls of the closed corridor. *She's gone!* Phosa could feel warmth and excitement surge all over her body at the thought of him. *Simon, all to myself!*

Phosa emerged from her bedroom into an empty corridor with her hair tied loosely behind her neck with frilled light blue ribbons that matched the tunic and silver-pressed sandals she had found in her room. Not wanting to loose any more time with Simon, she decided to forgo any cosmetics and hoped she wouldn't regret it later. The house was eerily quiet. Where is everyone? Phena had disappeared. And the servants that usually floated from room to room with linens, baskets, amphorae, and other household objects were nowhere to be seen. She followed the tiled floor to the end of the hallway, where it opened up into a courtyard and garden. *Still no one.* She turned her head to the left and observed the final wooden carts of the night as they awkwardly made their way past the house on the stoney streets outside. The front door was open, but Sebius was noticeably missing.

Phosa approached the atrium and walked the ten feet or so to the moneylending stall, and pressed her hand on the heavy wood door, assuming it would be easy to open. It wasn't. She pushed harder and gained a few inches. Her entire body froze when she heard the noise of heavy breathing mixed with female moans of pleasure. Disgusted, Phosa was ready to close the door and leave when she heard the woman's voice again, 'Simon! Oh, keep going! Do that again!"

At first, she assumed that two of the household slaves had made it to the stall before Simon and were enjoying themselves a little too much. But then she remembered that Phena had said Simon was waiting for her. She froze, mesmerized by the rhythmic noises she heard in the room.

A dreadful realization struck her with the force of a clay roof tile crashing down upon her. It can't be. It's not Simon. She knew she had to get in there and see. All the strength she lacked a few moments earlier came to her in a rush, and to her utter horror, the entirety of the scene was revealed to her. The truth is on display like dirty laundry hanging out a window. Two naked bodies lay interlocked on the dusty floor, one a stranger, the other someone she no longer wanted to know.

Phosa clenched her fists, fighting back tears of rage and betrayal. Angry and without saying anything, she stormed out of the bathroom stall, not concerned with her destination. She strode past the main entrance of the house and continued along the sidewalk, navigating through the bustling street. She passed two men dressed in matching uniforms, then a woman with her two servants in tow. Phosa rushed along, hiding herself behind her hood. The noise of merchant carts clashing against the pavement and horses whinnying in agony couldn't mask the sounds of that woman's pleasure as she...

She didn't know how long she had been walking when she finally stopped to catch her breath. She leaned against a nearby building and took deep breaths, trying to calm herself down. Suddenly, she felt a hand on her shoulder and jumped in surprise. Turning around, she saw Simon gazing down at her with concern etched on his face.

""Phosa! Wait! Phosa!" Phosa whipped herself away from his grasp and kept moving. *No, Simon. Just stop!* The sound of her name escaping his lips felt like a blade being thrust into her.

"Phosa! It's not safe for you out here. Come back!"

Still, she pressed on, not even sure if she cared about her own safety anymore. She crossed the intersection and passed a divinely smelling bakery, then a food stall and a wood craftsman. All of them going about their business, happily making a wage for their families. Their children. That's all she wanted in the world. A simple life with a family to love and care for. *What a fool I've been.* She thought, with courage enough to look back at the man who had consumed her every thought. *What a fool I am!* Phosa stopped, not able to walk any further.

"Phosa!" Simon yelled, "Come back to the house. I can explain everything."

"I will not hear it!"

"You must!"

"Must I?" Phosa couldn't look at him any longer. She pushed herself past him, determined to get away.

"Yes." His hands spread tightly all around her arm. She was stuck. "You don't understand."

"Get your hands off me!" She yelled, not caring if anyone was watching. She tried to wrench herself from his grip. "There are many things in life I don't understand, but that was not one of them."

"Oh, Phosa!"

"Stop it! Stop this, whatever it is!" She tried again to rest her arm on him, and this time, he loosened his grip. Not wanting to hear anything he had to say, she started walking again.
"Phosa, Please just come with me. Don't make me explain everything here in the middle of the street!" She didn't move, didn't care about his pride.

"I am betrothed to her." He whispered gently with regret."What?" Phosa's eyes widened in shock, and her entire body tensed as she looked at Simon's sad expression and slumped shoulders. Her surroundings blurred as she tried to process what he had just revealed to her.

"I'm sorry I didn't tell you before but..."

"But what??" The initial shock from his words had subsided, replaced with anger.

"I hoped to have it all terminated soon. My father said he could get me out of this."

She couldn't help but laugh. "Get you out of it? You looked quite ok with whatever arrangement this is..."

"She forced me! She said she would turn us all in as criminals if I didn't....Phosa! You have to believe me. She blackmailed me."

"So you had sex with her so that she would keep quiet."

"I had to. Phosa." He grabbed her again. His grasp seared her flesh. "Simon, you must let me be." She declared, departing from his life forever.

chapter seventeen

ARSONIST OR INNOCENT?

Heartheavy with betrayal, Phosa walked away from Simon without a backward glance. Her steps were filled with purpose, her mind made up. She needed time away from this deception, away from the pain that clawed at her insides. Ignoring Simon's pleas echoing behind her, she found herself walking aimlessly through the bustling streets of Rome. The city seemed to thrum with life, oblivious to the turmoil in her heart.

As she navigated the crowded pathways, Phosa's thoughts whirled around the image of Simon entangled with another woman. The realization that he had been promised to someone else all along seared through her like a white-hot iron. Finally, finding a secluded spot near the Tiber River, she sank down onto a weathered stone bench. The sound of water gently lapping against the riverbank provided a soothing backdrop to her tumultuous emotions. Lost in her thoughts, the warm sun casting a golden glow around her, Phosa felt a gentle hand on her shoulder. She turned slightly to see the nervous smile of Sarah, Sebius' slave girl.

"Sarah, what are you doing out here on your own?"

"Miss Tryphosa, the master would speak with you." *I just sat down!* She desperately wanted to refuse but knew she couldn't. Every single day, he made it clear how indebted they were to him. But still, Phosa didn't move.

"The master has made a decision, my lady." *A decision? About what?* She searched her mind, completely forgetting the promise he had made to her and her sister a few weeks ago. Will he support Phena in her project or not? And if yes, in what capacity? Phosa wasn't sure she really cared. Phena's idea of starting an orphanage really had little to do with her. It was her sister's dream. And right now, all of Phosa's dreams were broken into tiny pieces.

Reluctantly, Phosa accepted Sarah's assistance and got up from her resting place next to the water. For a moment, she seriously contemplated telling Sebius of the scene that she had witnessed earlier. But that would force her to recall it and perhaps even cement their betrothal. Neither outcome was desirable.

Phosa followed closely behind Sarah as she weaved through the streets with ease. She had clearly walked this route many times. *Perhaps she has sought out time to herself by the water.* Phosa hoped so. She couldn't help but wonder what Sarah thought of her life as a slave. Did she have dreams? Hopes to be freed one day? To wed? The sweetness in her face betrayed none of those hopes. *Perhaps Sebius is a fair master.*

She entered the house through the atrium. Sarah brought a large stone bowl of water for her to wash her feet in and then escorted her to Sebius' private office. Sebius stood tall and statuesque, his gaze fixed out the window at the lively street. He wore a pristinely pressed white tunic with a brilliant blue sash dropped across his shoulder, a symbol of his wealth and position. Phosa noticed that his hands were blackened and that there were pieces of parchment scattered across his desk.

He turned slowly as if he hadn't heard her walk in. "Oh, Phosa. My apologies. Please excuse the mess. I've been meeting with clients all morning." Suddenly, she felt nervous. *Why isn't Phena here, too? Surely he should tell her first? Or was there something else he wanted to talk about? Does he already know about Simon?* She felt her heart racing in her chest as she watched him pour a cup of wine for himself and motion for her to sit on a couch opposite him. She desperately wanted to decline but felt like she couldn't. She was a guest in his house, and he had the power. Phosa calmly lowered herself, trying not to reveal any of the uncertainty clouding her mind.

"Phosa, my dear. I trust you had a restful sleep?"

"Oh yes, thank you, sir." She replied without thinking.

"Sarah has been treating you well?"

"Yes, thank you."

"And my son?"

"What about Your son?"

"He's been treating you well?" Not exactly.

"Yes, I suppose so, sir."

"Excellent. I've asked you to come see me for several reasons. First, Simon reported to me today that you missed your shift in our stall."

Simon! He told his father I was absent. What cheek!

"Oh, yes, sir. My apologies. I'm afraid I could not engage in my duties this morning." Phosa answered, racking her brain for a more specific reason why she couldn't.

"And why not?"

"I uh, well, sir, I just started my courses." *God forgive me for lying.*

"Oh, yes. Well, in that case, I'll make an allowance." Sebius said, downing the rest of his wine. "But remember, if you are to be a part of this household, you must fulfill your duties. And next time, please inform your maid of your, uh, condition."

"Yes, sir." Phosa returned, feeling quite awkward. "And there was something else, sir?"

His face turned slightly sour as if his wine had been tainted. He stood up and returned to his place of power behind his desk.

"Yes, I've received a report from a member of my household that I wanted to check with you before I mention it to Phena." Phosa nodded, signaling for him to continue. "This report states that you and your sister are murderers and arsonists." Phosa could feel every muscle in her body tighten up and her stomach's violent revolt against such a claim. Panic took hold of her heart and mind, thinking about what was at stake if her rebuttal wasn't compelling enough. Tongue-tied and dry-mouthed, she started her reply over and over and then finally pushed the words to her mouth.

"Sir, I want to ease your mind. My sister and I are not arsonists or murderesses."

"Go on." His eyes revealed nothing of his thoughts, just cool determination.

"As you know, our apartment building burned down just over a month ago. We did not set the fire. My sister and I managed to get out of our apartment and into the corridor but collapsed there. When I recovered, our servant Rusticus stood before us."

"Rusticus? That name sounds familiar. Does he have other names?"

"No, just Rusticus. He helped us get to the top of the stairs that led down ot the street, but then he fell with Phena over his shoulders. "

"Oh, how dreadful. Phena was obviously all right?"

"Yes, she came to within a few minutes, and Rusticus was awake, but he couldn't move." Phosa's emotions overcame her, closing up her throat so that she could hardly breathe, let alone speak. The image of Rusticus lying there still haunted her nights and now would haunt her days.

"I'm sorry, Phosa. To make you relive this. You don't have to..." Unexpectedly, Sebius moved back to his seat across from her, a look of empathy and compassion on his face.

 "No, I will prove our innocence." She bravely started again, "I, we, left him there. He told us to go and live. I desperately tried to find someone to help us drag him out of the building, but the crowd was against us, shouting all manner of curses and accusations. We ran. We left him!"

The tears started to flow freely down her face as the guilt of what they'd done overwhelmed her. I left him! My friend! I left him there to die! I told him I'd find someone to help! And I just ran!

She barely noticed Sebius' strong arms wrap around her as she sobbed. "There, there. I'm sorry. I believe you." Sebius's voice was as gentle as his touch, and he combed her hair with his hand.

"What's this?" Phena stood in the doorway, looking confused and slightly angry. Phosa sat up and clumsily wiped the tears from her face with the end of her tunic. She recognized her sister's voice, but the figure in front of her was a stranger. She wore a long, flowing tunic in a vibrant lilac hue, held together by a golden clasp on her right shoulder. Her hair was styled in loose curls, giving off an air of sophistication and elegance.

"Phena, my darling! You look beautiful, my dear. Please come in." Phosa was startled to see Sebius' eyes so quickly change from stoic dignity to gentle passion. "I was just comforting your sister. She has a lot on her mind. But not to worry, right Phosa?"

"That's right, sir." Phena graciously nodded and strode confidently through the room, heading straight for the couch without sparing a glance at her sister.

"I'm so glad you've joined us. Now we can share our news."

"News?" Phosa asked, confused.

"Yes, sister, Sebius and I have made excellent progress towards our mutual goals." That means nothing, and you know it.

"I'm excited to tell you that Sebius has found a building that we can transform into an orphanage, and the lawyers have drawn up all of the required documents for the sale of the property and the beginning of our joint endeavors!" Phena's face radiated light as she spoke of her future.

"Yes, my dear." Sebius agreed, standing up to stand far too close to Phena. He gently took hold of both her hands and, in one slow-smooth motion, passionately kissed each of her fingers. Phena stood by, not only allowing such a display but seemingly enjoying it.

"There is now only one further contract to draw up."

"Pray, do tell."

"Sister, Sebius and I are to be married."

Phosa sat frozen in her seat. She could see nothing. And feel nothing. All was still except the rushing beat of her heart. Her fingers tingled, and her ears registered the sound. But that was all.

"Phosa!" In an instant, her sister's harsh voice projected her back to reality. She was suddenly overcome by the exhaustion of her circumstances. Glaring at Phena, she felt a mixture of betrayal, hurt, and righteous anger consume her. How could her sister, who claimed to have no interest in marriage, even consider such an offer from Sebius?

"Phosa, you have to say something."

"What am I supposed to say?"

"I don't know, congratulations or something? And if you can't be happy for my marriage, at least be happy the orphanage is going to happen."

"Phosa couldn't take it anymore. Is that all you care about? Your house for the unwanted?"

"Now, Phosa," Sebius's authoritative voice boomed. "Don't you want your sister's scheme to succeed?" *How can I say no to that?*

"Of course, I guess."

"Well, this is the only way. Why am I taking risks myself, making your sister my wife? She is neither Jewish nor rich. What is left of my Jewish connections are likely to shun me."

Phosa's frustration reached its peak. "Wasn't it just a month ago that you said all those things mattered little to you? Now, you use them to show how gracious you are!" Phosa remarked sarcastically, her voice laced with bitterness. There was nothing more to say.

"Phosa! How dare you speak to him like that!"

"It's all right, my love. She will come to terms with our decision."

Phena's expression shifted, and a flicker of uncertainly crossed her features as she met Phosa's intense gaze. For a moment, her facade of indifference crumbled, revealing a glimpse of vulnerability underneath. "Phosa, you must understand," she began, her voice tinged with a hint of defensiveness. "This is not about me. It's about ensuring a future for us and for those lost children still living in poverty outside the city."

"I am glad you want to help the children, but Phena, your plans have nothing to do with me."

"Phosa!" Sebius stepped forward and leaned against his desk, his eyes caring but authoritative. "Let me explain something to you. As an unmarried young woman with no male guardian, you are defenseless and vulnerable according to Roman law. You are a part of all this, because by marrying your sister I mean to give you a place in this world." *I'm not going to like when he's about to say, am I?* "I have arranged a marriage for you as well. His name is Julianus Titus Aurelius; he is a well-connected son of an ex-praetor who has just returned from the provinces. He is, of course, from a Christian family."

Phosa stood there completely speechless. "What?" In a flash, she realized what this really meant. Even if she wanted to, which she wasn't sure she did, she would never be with Simon now. "But you have no power over me. I'm not your daughter or..." She tried to sound reasonable and intelligent, but her voice faltered under the weight of her boiling emotions.

"Phosa, as it stands, the Roman authorities consider you and your sister dead. And if they ever learned that you survived the fire and your trek outside of the city, then they would be looking for you. So, regardless of whether or not I have the right to be your guardian, I will be. We cannot consult Roman law over this, and you cannot live as a single woman your whole life. We will simply change your name and have our scribe draw up a new appears for you. You'll be ready for matrimony in less than six weeks.

"I most certainly won't be! Father always said I could decide! I want to decide!" It was at this moment that she realized that even though she was still traumatized by his betrayal, she wanted to be with Simon. Finally, she let out a bloodcurdling scream of frustration, picked up what looked like a very expensive case, and cast it across the room, narrowly missing her sister's head.

Phena's calm demeanor only felt like salt on her wound. "Phosa, this is all you've ever wanted! Marriage! Why do you refuse it now?"

"Because I want to choose, I want a say for once! Is that so difficult to understand?"

"No, indeed it is not." Sebius' voice was surprisingly gentle. "But we live in dangerous times. We must keep you safe, and the only way to do this is to see you married. You'll see Julianus is a wonderful match."

"No! No! I won't do it!"

"Phosa! It has been decided! Although we have agreed to allow you some time to process this. You will meet your betrothed on your wedding day, which will be in precisely six weeks."

Six weeks....and my life is over! Phosa felt completely powerless, and she was.

Taking a deep breath to calm her emotions, Phosa spoke with a mixture of determination and pleading. "Phena, can you truly feel good about what you're doing to me? to yourself?"

Phena looked at her as if she were speaking another language. Then he walked over to her future husband, who was still standing behind his desk. Her hands gently caressed his face, and he willingly leaned in to offer her hip lips. Phosa stood there awkwardly, wondering where her sister had gone for his seductive woman n front of her was surely not her. Phena released herself from Sebius' grip and turned their attention back to Phosa.

"Listen, sister; the Lord has instructed me to do everything that I am doing. I am sure of that. He has placed Sebius in our lives for a purpose. So I am going to marry him and do the Lord's work. As for you, we are merely doing what our father should have done before he died. If anything, you should be angry at his reckless failure to provide for you himself."

Phena's words sounded like a mumbled cacophony of nonsense. Unable to contain the storm raging inside her for even one more second, Phosa abruptly turned her back on Phena and stormed out.

chapter eighteen

NO SAY IN THE MATTER

Phosa stormed through the streets of Rome, everything around her a blur, her hood pulled tightly around her face, shielding her from the curious glances of passers-by. Temples to gods and goddesses that she her family used to worship towered above her, their grandeur lost in the heat of her anger. The streets of Rome were crowded and chaotic; colorful garments and animated gestures only added to the sense of chaos. The scent of freshly baked bread and roasted meats wafted through the air, mixing with the stench of horse manure and sweat. But Phosa was too consumed by her emotions to notice the usual smells of the bustling city.

The rough fabric of her hood scratched against her face, a constant reminder of her turmoil. Her fists clenched tightly, nails digging into her skin as she marched on, ignoring the throbbing pain.

It seemed to her that everyone in her life was betraying her all at once, first Simon and now Phena. *How could she forget me? How could she claim for herself what she has always dreamed of?* She continued to walk through the streets, passing people holding baskets, ladies walking with their servants, and men speaking loudly with their hands.

As she turned onto Via Riale, she knew that her destination was due south. The river. She'd found some solace there this morning, she'd hopefully find it again.

The sight of the rushing water calmed her spirits. She left the dirt and rubble of the Roman streets and scaled the unkept path to the river bed. She didn't care that her tunic would inevitably get muddy. She didn't care that it wasn't proper for her to be outside by herself. She didn't even care if some ruffian came up behind her wielding a knife. She needed this.

She lowered herself into the mud and watched the river go by. She had intentionally chosen a place where there was no crossing, a private place where no one would see her. She let herself slip into a quiet peace, focusing on the sound of the rapids. But just as she closed her eyes to gather her scattered emotions, a voice interrupted the tranquility she sought.

"Tryphosa," came a soft, hesitant voice. A voice that she would recognize anywhere. She stayed in her place, immobile and unsure. Did she want to hear him out? Did she want to look at his beautiful face again? Did she have a choice? Phosa's eyes snapped open to see Simon standing a few paces away, clinging to the hillside. His perfect face was a mixture of concern and regret. The sweetness of his green eyes pierced her soul. And the nagging quiver of his lips brought up a longing she had hoped was extinguished.

"Simon, I...." The words were not coming to her.

"No, Tryphosa, please let me speak." He climbed gracefully down the hill and fell on his knees at her side, plunging himself into the mud.
"I love you. I've loved you from the moment I saw you. I knew I had to have you."

Phosa could barely concentrate on his words. The air was heavy with the earthy scent of the mud beneath them and the crisp smell of the nearby river. Mixed in was the subtle, intoxicating scent of Simon - a blend of leather and a hint of pine that always seemed to linger around him.

"Simon, please don't do this." As Simon reached out to touch her hand, Phosa could feel the gentle yet firm grip of his ink-stained fingers. She fought with herself, wishing she could bask in that moment and just enjoy his touch. But her pragmatic mind stopped her. She awkwardly refused him and held her hands in front of her. SHe only stared into the wadding waters of the Riber, wishing for a simpler life.

"No, wait, there's more. I will never hurt you again! I promise! I've already spoken to my father; he is going to call off my betrothal. It's over. Finished."

Yes but mine has just begun! Exacerbated by her situation, she sprang to her feet, her face flushed with frustration.

"Simon, that doesn't change what I saw, which, if I'm honest, completely shattered me. But even that doesn't matter anymore!"

"What do you mean it doesn't matter anymore? It does! All I can do is beg your forgiveness."

The sincerity and desperation she saw in his eyes were heart-wrenching. *Maybe UI can get out of my betrothal? I've already flat-o. t refused. There has to be a way.* Her heart was torn between what she felt and what she knew she should do. But despite her strong determination to reject him as she had promised, the yearning in his gaze was like a rope pulling her towards him. A smile crawled onto her face as her spirits began to lift. *She's my sister. Maybe I can convince her. Beg her!*

She turned to him, her hand reaching up to gently trace his beautiful face. She wanted to etch the feeling of his slightly chapped lips against hers into her memory forever. Her heart raced with anticipation as she longed for his embrace. Like a drowning person clinging to a lifeline, she pressed her lips against his, and he responded eagerly. The sensation of his warm lips on hers was pure bliss. As he tenderly explored her body and pulled her closer to him, she felt like she was on fire in the best possible way. He caressed her breasts and slipped his hand under her tunic, exploring the hidden depths within. For a few sweet moments, they were lost in each other's touch, oblivious to any onlookers. Then her wits returned to her. She remembered that she couldn't have him. Ever. Not now. She pulled away from his embrace and stood before him.

"We can't do this."

"Come on, Phosa, I promise you, I'm yours. I'm only yours. I want you to be my wife!"

"I can't I'm betrothed."

"What? What do you mean?"

"Your father has arranged a match for me!"

"What? Are you serious? Who is he? Why would they do that?" Despite the turmoil of the movement, she couldn't suppress a smile at how vexed he seemed to be. "

"For obvious reasons Simon, I need a husband, so they say. "

I'll, I'll tell him he can't. I'll tell him I want to marry you."

"You think that will do anything?"

"Well, at least..."

"No, you'll only humiliate both of us. It's already decided. I am marrying Julianius."

"No! Phosa, I love you. I want to marry you!"

Phosa's heart was breaking all over again. She was ready to forgive him for his betrayal, but she knew this marriage would only cause her to be an ever-present part of her sister's household. She wanted to be rid of her, not be her understudy.

"Simon, this is the end."

Seconds after the words slipped out of her mouth, she regretted them. Before she could change her mind, she raced up the side of the side of the hill and onto the street. And she didn't look back.

The sun's glow was fading to a distant memory and the heat of the day was replaced by a calming breeze. Phosa dreaded returning to Simon's father's house, but she had nowhere else to go. She intended to slip into the back entrance, through the servant's quarters, and straight to her room, completely unseen. There she would quietly figure out how she could escape her current meaningless bondage.

Phosa turned the corner onto Via Entare, a stone's throw from the vast green-painted doors of the stables. She quietly approached the gates and made sure that the small rectangular watchmen's hatch was not open. As her hand grasped the brass ring attached to the door, she overheard two men whispering in the shadowy alleyway across the street. They were both of medium height and wearing dirty scraps of clothes that only a slave would be caught in. They were hunched over and leaning into the plastered buildings.

"Listen, now is not the right time," one of them said. She thought she recognized the man's voice, although it was slightly altered. More scratchy than she remembered. *But that's impossible.*

"The gods will strike me down if I don't report them today!" the other replied.

Feeling exposed, Phosa cautiously retreated further down the street, making sure she was out of sight but could still clearly hear their conversation. She waited for the men to put her fears to bed.

"I want Sebius to get what he deserves!" the unfamiliar male voice said. Then, in a split second, their exchange escalated as the blade of a knife was exposed and violently pressed upon the man's throat. Trembling, the victim raised his hands in submission; his lips moved, but Phosa could not hear his words.

The mysterious man holding the knife retaliated by roughly grabbing his curly hair with savagery. "Do you doubt me?" He pushed them violently against the wall. His hood was pulled down in t, revealing a deep and jagged burn scar that ran from his temple to his jawline. Phosa gasped at the sight of it. *Rusticus! You're alive?* The man turned his face towards her hiding place and then returned his attention to the man in front of him. But she was sure he didn't see her.

"He will get what he deserves! But I have my own vengeance to exact! Those girls ruined my life, and they will pay dearly for it." Rusticus released his prisoner and sprinted down the alley, disappearing into the shadows.

Phosa's face drained of color as she trembled, her body rigid with terror. *He's gonna kill us!* With all of her heart, she wanted to believe that Jesus would protect them, but old fears returned; old stories threw themselves onto her heart.

All at once, a rush of fear flooded through her body, causing her firm belief to waver and struggle like an injured creature. He said we would pay dearly. She trembled at the thought of her demise and looked up at the now vacant space where the two men had just plotted her death.

I have to warn Phena.

chapter nineteen

LOOKING FOR YOU

THREE WEEKS LATER

The summer flowers bloomed and then withered under the unbearably hot August sun. Phosa struggled to find a moment to alert her sister about the covert assembly she had stumbled upon, but with her wedding just around the corner, there was simply no time. An army of well-dressed caterers, florists, tailors, and seamstresses were in and out of the house, frantic to put together a party that would once again endear Sebius and his family to the Jewish community. Tables were set up in the garden with long, flowing, embroidered white clothes with blue tassels hanging down the sides. Magnificently crafted menorahs were brought from the nearest synagogue, a sign of renewed favor.

Suddenly, she heard the sound of many sandals dancing along the tile floors, coming from the direction of the office. "Oh, Phosa!" Her sister yelled, followed by a swarm of four ladies and one male servant holding a tablet.

"Oh, Phinus, don't write this down, please." She instructed as if she'd been born a lady of a great household. "There you are, sister! I've been looking for you!"

"I've been looking for you too, actually."

"Never mind that. In two days time, I will be a lady of the house! Just imagine that!" She said dreamily. "And, there's so much to do! Can you round up the rest of the housemaids? The dining room needs to be scrubbed and adorned, and the chambers need to be made up for the guests. Oh, and call on the gardener, he'll need to do some weeding."

"Oh, my lady." Phinus stepped in hesitatingly. "The gardener was let go some weeks ago."

"That's become obvious. Hire another."

"Yes, my lady."

"Phena?" Phosa raised her voice to compete with all the chatter.

"Yes?"

"I really have something I need to tell you."

"Can't it wait? And Phosa, you've been neglecting your scribe duties in the shop. Sebius expects you to take that up immediately if you wish to remain in this household."

"What do you mean if I wish to remain in this household?"

"You heard me, " Her sister quickly retorted as her eyes poured over the wax tablet in front of her. She's pretending to read. Of course, she is. I can play this game too, sister.

"Sister, I regret to inform you I will not be taking up my duties as a scribe."

“Excuse me?”

“I have news that will interrupt all business and all future plans for this household.”

“Leave my presence immediately.” She ordered with a wave of her hand. For a moment Phosa was sure her sister was talking to her, but then saw the servants behind her begin to retreat.

“Sister! Do you not see what you've become?” Phosa's emotionally heightened voice echoed in the atrium, turning heads of servants passing by.

“You no longer even talk about those children! What of your orphanage?”

“Do not speak to me like that!”

“I will! Someone has to!” Phosa violently shrugged off the servants as they attempted to restrain her.

“Sister, will you not hear me out? Do you not even care for this household that you suddenly have ambitions to run?” Phena stopped. The determination in her eyes turned to sadness. "I care deeply for this household, Tryphosa, but your wild behavior will only bring shame upon us. It is time you learned your place. It's no secret you run off to the river whenever you can." she stated coldly.

“I must tell you that there is someone who means to harm us and your precious Sebius!”

“Do not be naive. Men of great wealth such as Sebius expect such things.”

“So I am to keep such reports to myself?”

"I really do not care what you do with yourself, Phosa. You clearly do not wish to take any instruction or obey those in authority over you. Just leave me."

Phosa was not in an obedient mood and remained where she was. "Ok, sister. I shall leave. I have a business to conduct. But I do not wish to see you."

With that Phena rushed away, her polished shoes clattering along the tiled floor as she disappeared down a hallway. Phosa's legs threatened to give out. She sank onto the cold cement bench behind her, numbness spreading through her heart like frost.

How do I make her listen to me? She has to know...about Rusticus.

His words flooded her mind again, the venom in them haunted her. *Who could blame him for wanting revenge? We left him to die. A horrible horrible death. And now he wears an angry scar that shows he'll never stop until he has what. he wants. Revenge!*

She rushed to her room and fell headlong onto her bed, where the floodgates were opened and her tears fell freely. "Lord, are you still with us?" Phosa whispered threw her tears.

I am here. I will always be here.

Phosa raised her tear-soaked face from the now wet blankets and looked around, expecting a noisy, well-versed servant to come to see if she was all right. But there was no one. A still, small voice whispered again.

Phosa, you are mine. Remember that.

Again Phosa looked around. Then she realized what was happening and felt a warmth she had never felt before covered her entire body. In an instant, fresh air filled her lungs and her anguish was lifted.

I know now, that no matter what happens, my hope is in you. Not my safety.

chapter twenty

SPIES IN OUR MIDST

A much-needed rest granted her temporary reprieve from the pains of her existence but promptly returned when she opened to her.

"Miss? Miss? Are you awake?" It was the sweet and gentle voice of her maid, Sarah.

"Yes, I'm awake."

"Miss, I am reminding you that there is a meeting for our brothers and sisters in one hour."

"Thank you." She sat up in her bed, pulled back her disheveled hair, and took in a deep breath of fresh air. Pushing back the blankets, she realized she was not thinking about how she could impress Simon, or indeed anyone else. And she actually wanted to go. She wanted to be among her brothers and sisters, to be encouraged by the peace and joy that she remembered was so evidently written upon their faces.

Phosa opened the door of her chamber and immediately heard the joyful chorus of her brothers and sisters chatting in the main outdoor living room where most of their gatherings were held. She started walking down the canopied corridor, her palms dry and her heart lightened by the mysterious yet sweet whispers she heard,

Daughter, I love you.
I'll never leave.
You're mine.

Comforted, Phosa rounded the corner leading to the great outdoor room. She first heard a tearing noise and then was yanked backward. The hem of her yellow tunic caught the hinge of a nearby cabinet that had once housed the previous family's household gods.

"Be careful now." warned a man with a long white beard, protruding nose, and kind brown eyes. His clothes were made of plain linen and looked filthy as if he had been on a long journey.

"Let me help you with that." He bent over and carefully lifted the smooth silk material from the hinge unscathed.

"Thank you, my lord."

"No, no! Not my Lord, there is but one Lord. And I am not He."

"Well, thank you anyway." She returned awkwardly.

The man only rose to his medium height, smiled, and started to walk towards the now quieting assembly, and then unexpectedly, he turned to her again, "Young lady, there are snares everywhere you turn. Be watchful!" His words stayed with her long after the sound had left her ears. She wasn't sure what he meant, but she knew it would be important.

Still pondering the curious man's words, Phosa confidently glided into the room where all were patiently waiting for the host's arrival. She avoided the temptation to scan the crowd for Simon's familiar face. Instead, she met the cautious light blue eyes of a caring middle-aged plebeian woman with dark brown hair tied back at the nap of her neck and a long light green ankle-length tunic. Phosa remembered her from the last time, Sharon. She gestured for her to sit beside her on one of the many couches.

"Sharon, thank you!"

"You are most welcome, dear. Have you been well?"

Phosa wasn't sure how to answer that. *Yes and no. Yes, I am fine now. No I wasn't fine before.*

"I am well. Thank you. And how is your son, Andreaus?"

"Yes, that is his name! You remembered. He is well and will start his assignment soon."

"Assignment?" Phosa asked, intrigued despite the growing number of shushes she was receiving.

"Yes, he's been assigned to Julius Fortus' regiment in the Arena."

"Nero's great water arena, you mean?"

"Yes. Please pray." Then Sharon's attention flew towards the open garden where Sebius and Simon were speaking with the door guard, Jarius.

"Do you think that is him?" Sharon asked, her eyes fixed on the tall lanky frame of Sebius' North African slave, Jarius.

"Him? What do you mean?" Phosa was only partially listening. The garden was buzzing with activity, as brothers and sisters filed in and took their seats. The meeting was set to begin soon.

"Did you not receive your letter? Sebius warned us all that there is a slave in his household that is reporting back to Nero." Phosa's eyes changed in an instant from calm to agitated. *What is she talking about? Reporting back to Nero?*

In an instant, it felt like a hand had reached into her chest and squeezed her heart. A slave in Sebius' household? She knew about Rusticus. Now it seems like there is a whole network. Feeling utterly surrounded, and reminded that her sister had all but abandoned her just hours ago, she was sure that she would collapse. A wave of panic washed over her, a dangerous emotion that could incite fear-driven chaos.

"Sharon, I believe this isn't something we should be whispering about here..." She was trying desperately to be strong.

"Everyone knows, dear. Did you not... Aren't you the future sister-in-law of the master?" Her gaze dropped to the stone walkway, as if ashamed that she had been the one to tell her.

Yes, I am

Sebius barked one more order at his servant and gestured for him to go back to the front of the house, while a silent and distracted Simon stood still. Seeing him again, standing there in his stoic manner, his shining brown curls illuminated by the candlelight, his gentle brown eyes beautiful even as they appeared dazed and burdened. She longed to go to him, even as a friend, and embrace him. She wanted to share in the burdens that he so obviously carried. For a brief moment she allowed herself to remember how his lips had felt on hers.

The sensation of a thousand tiny sparks erupting along her spine was etched into her memory, the embers still lingering within her body. She forced her thoughts from that cherished moment. Their love was an impossible one. She was still betrothed to a stranger, and she was sure that in no time, his father would arrange a match for him as well. They could never be together.

"Welcome, Welcome friends!" Phosa turned her attention to the master who stood beside her love. Sebius' jovial frame bounded towards the back of the room where Phena was quietly whispering with a fellow lady. She was wearing a humble tunic of lightly colored pink with a slightly rusted clasp at her shoulder. Phosa couldn't help but notice her new hairstyle, a modest bun in the style of Roman ladies. *How changed you are.* He stood before her and held out his hand, in a chivalric program. "Rise, my beloved, and stand with me before our guests". She noticeably blushed, held out her hand, and bid him to kiss it. Phosa could see a wide grin run across his face as he led her to the front of the assembly.

Still holding her hand, he began, "It is our pleasure to host you in our home as we worship our Saviour and read aloud the scriptures. Before we sing our first song, we are happy to present to you another very special guest. You'll all have remembered our guest from the last meeting, Rufus. Well, he has made his way back to the church he leads in North Africa. And since his departure, we have been blessed to receive one even more intimately known to our Saviour. We have been waiting for, nay counting on, his arrival for years, and he has finally made it to the city of Rome."

As he spoke, the elderly man who had freed her from the terrible hinge, came forward. *A special guest, hmm?* Phosa couldn't help but think he didn't look overly special.

"Thank you Sebius! Please find a seat with your lovely lady." Phena caught in a persistent blush, curtseyed and sat down with her almost husband.

"Ladies, and gentlemen! Brothers and sisters! I greet you with the unconditional eternal love of Christ Jesus our Lord. I am Peter."

This pronouncement lifted up a gaggle of stunned *awhhs* and *ohhs*, and spontaneous conversations throughout the crowd.

"As Sebius mentioned, you have been waiting for my arrival for years. Here I am. I have come to minister to our brothers and sisters in Rome through words of truth and encouragement. First amongst my encouragement is to stand firm in the faith that at first saved you. You all know that these are hard times and that even harder times are expected to come. But do not be afraid, for our Lord and Saviour has overcome the world." Peter stopped speaking for a moment, and closed his eyes, even as the crowd hung on his every word.

"I can still remember the day my Jesus said those very words to me. And the truth of them has sustained me. The dangers that we face in this world are of no consequence. What we should fear is our fate in the next world. So stand firm. You have been given the way, the truth, and the life. There is no other that can give you that. Where can you go to find those?"

"No-where!" Dozens of voices shouted in unison.

""Yes! Amen! Nowhere is right! I can find no purpose for life, except in Christ!" Joy brimmed out of Phosa from a deep place in her soul, like a bottle with too much wine in it.

In a moment of sincere passion, Phosa could not help but shout, "We shall stand firm! Though the lions leap upon us, we will put our hope in Jesus and await his eternal life!"

"Praise the Lord! Amen!" Peter bent over and slowly took his seat on the couch again, his age fully on display for the group of followers.

"Thank you, Peter!" Sebius said, standing in front of the group again. "You will be among us for quite some time, yes?"

"Until the Lord wills my departure."

"Yes, of course. So you'll have ample opportunity to speak with him later on. Now, I'd like to deliver some news for our community. First, my new sister Phosa, has been working on transcribing additional copies of Paul's recent letter to our community here in Rome. Phosa, please tell us how this project is coming along."

Phosa's hand fidgeted nervously as she ran it through her hair, causing the neat bun that Sarah had painstakingly crafted to become slightly disheveled. "I Uh-" She was completely aware of all the eyes on her and found it difficult to form her words.

"Phosa, why don't you stand up?"

Oh God, what torture! Phosa thought to herself, reluctantly obeying the master. "I uh, yes I have been working on the letters. There are four copies thus far. I will continue transcribing further copies."

"The goal is to have a copy for all the house churches in Rome. Is that right, Phosa?"

"Yes, Lord that is right."

"Thank you Phosa, and while you are standing, we want to congratulate you on your recent betrothal and marriage which is coming soon, isn't it?" She smiled nervously towards her future brother in law, her eyes diverting to Simon who did not hide his dread.

"Yes, thank you Sebius." Before she was asked another question, Phosa fell back into her seat. All eyes stayed on her until Sebius continued.

"Ok, we have some more news-"

"What of the spy?" Yelled a young woman sitting behind Phena.

"Yeah! Are we safe here?" Another woman called out in an anxious tone. Once again, Phosa's eyes slipped past Sebius, to Simon who by now had retreated to the far side of the gathering close to the tablinum. The look of him almost took her breath away, his chestnut curls traced the edges of his cleanly shaven face. His deep brown eyes were pools of contemplation. She couldn't help but rest her eyes upon him, knowing he, too, felt nervous and even nauseous at the mention of their dangers. He stood still as a statue, his arms folded, and his face revealing nothing. She knew these signs to mean that he was uncomfortable and desperate to keep up the image he'd worked hard to portray. A steadfast Christian who would never falter, even in the arena.

Then her gaze instinctively moved to a man shot up like a lightning bolt from amongst the crowd. His deep brown tunic swayed this way and that with his movements. *Thomas, I think.* Phosa thought to herself, remembering his golden blond hair, the deep emerald of his eyes, and his gentle yet firm features from the last meeting.

"Yes, Thomas? Do you have something to say?"

"Yes, thank you Sebius. I just want to remind you, brothers, and sisters, of what the great apostle Peter has just said to us. We must stand firm in Christ! He is our strength when we are being hunted. He is our hiding place when we are not safe."

"Thank you, brother. Yes, for all of you who are Jewish among us, you'll know that the Psalmist often referred to the LORD as a strong fortress in times of trouble. And we must put out hope in Him, not our circumstances."

"Hear! Hear!" The group roared.

Sebius held up his right hand to silence the crowd. "I can see that you have all received your note from my couriers, that we suspect there is at least one spy in our household that is reporting to Nero's personal investigative team."

"How did you come to suspect a member of your household?" A brother whom Phosa had never met asked from the middle of the crowd.

"Good question. One particular slave in my household was caught carrying a letter that included incriminating evidence against myself and members of his community."

"What did you do with him?" A woman at the back of the garden shouted.

"He received twenty lashes and returned to my household." *Great, so now he likely holds ill will.* "He is constantly monitored and has shown enough good behavior and his renewed loyalty to be allowed outside the house."

"So the threat has been decimated?" The sound of voices raised in excitement and joyful chatter blended together.

"No, not exactly." Their voices quieted again. "Just yesterday, I found anti-Christo drawings on the walls within the servant's quarters, and I have reports from loyal servants who have seen their fellows meeting with dangerous vagabonds and runaway slaves in the bar just a few doors down. Before you ask what I've done about that, I must admit that I have done nothing. I do not wish to strip my servants of all their luxuries."

"So you would endanger us!"

"Just cast out all your servants and get new ones!"

"Yeah, or kill them!"

"Wait, a second. Who said just kill them?" Sebius' stern shout rang through the house. The room fell into a tense silence, the group of listeners held their breath and shifted their gaze from Sebius to the short bald man who stepped forward, his head bowed down with guilt.

"Brother, I do not pretend to understand why you would suggest such a thing."

Phosa could only hear the intensified breathing of the man, his lips closed and his head bowed.

"Let it be said that we as a community will never condone such a recommendation! We are called to love; to turn the other cheek. It shocks me to hear any of you advocate such violence! We are not pagans. We are not even Romans anymore! We are Christians. You are not who you used to be." Sebius gently gestured for the man to sit back down.

"But what will you do?"

"I will continue to have those servants watched. And I will have one of you assigned to disciple them in the ways of Christ."

What?! Not sure what she thought of that, Phosa looked around the room and witnessed the ensuing chaos. Men and women raised their voices against Sebius, indignant at his proclamation.

"You can't put us in such danger!"

"Yeah, they'll hand us over!"

"You would see the death of us all!"

Phosa's stomach churned as memories of the night of the fire flooded her mind, and the harsh words of those who wanted to harm her replayed in her head. Arsonist, they had called her. She struggled to keep down the rising nausea. *Vapulabis! Incendiariae!* The words echoed in her mind. She could still feel their murderous eyes all over her. Phosa forced herself away from that haunting memory and turned her eyes toward Peter, the rock. He stood, his posture towering and commanding, his expression neutral yet powerful.
"You respond with shock and fury at our brother's instruction. But you should not. He has instructed you as Jesus Christ Himself would have. You don't seem to understand that our entire mission in life is to disciple the lost and share the hope of our perfect Saviour, Jesus Christ, with the world. And that includes Romans who want to kill us. Check your hearts and go."

The room around her seemed to freeze until all she could hear was the pounding of her heart in her chest. This mountain felt insurmountable. Their doom was sealed. Even the comforting words of Peter, the rock, were not enough to strangle the fears that lay in wait for her.

What does Phena think of all this? Does she fear as I do? The look of resolved confidence and strength that she saw her sister emulating from across the room was surely just duty, not genuine. *Or maybe she is just stronger than I am.*

Then a hunched over dark hooded figure coming from the unlit hallway caught her eye. He had come from the direction of the slaves quarters, and was gingerly making his way towards the crowd gathered in the garden. He must have sensed her gaze, for in a moment of recklessness he looked up and revealed a hideous scar,a scar that had since haunted her dreams and stalked her days.

chapter twenty-one
THE MEMORY OF SMOKE

Rusticus. He's here. Despite the unease she felt rising in her throat, she knew she had to get to him. To tell him she was sorry for everything. If there was even a small chance that he would listen it was worth it. She kept her eyes on him as she weaved through the crowd of shifting believers, some staying behind to talk and others heading towards the open front door and the bustling chaos of the streets of Rome.

"Excuse me, pardon me. Thank you. Please let me through." As graciously as she could, she passed between people talking, avoided toes in unprotected sandals, all the while her eyes fixed of the hunched over form that had retreated into a side room off of the garden.

She finally escaped the throng of people and stood on the cement walkway that lined the garden.

"Phosa! What did you think about…"

"Simon, sorry not now. I–"

"My lady, do you wish for some refreshments?" Sarah asked, standing behind her with a tray of sweetmeats.

"No, no, please let me be."

She walked past both of them and didn't look back to see their confused expressions. *I have to find him before someone else does.* She bounded towards the room that she had seen him go into, the door partially closed behind him. She took a deep breath, closed her eyes, and whispered a prayer, and then, in one brisk motion, she opened the door. She grabbed a lit torch from the hallway and entered. *This is by far the dumbest thing I've ever done.*

Phosa's heart pulsed in her ears, drowned out by the deafening silence of the empty room. The flickering torch cast eerie shadows against the walls, playing tricks on her eyes. She took hesitant steps further into the room, her sandals whispering against the stone floor. Just as doubt began to cloud her mind, a soft rustling noise reached her ears. Phosa spun around, her heart leaping to her throat. There, in the far corner, shrouded in darkness, was a figure crouched low to the ground.

"Rusticus?" Phosa's voice trembled with a mixture of fear and remorse.

The figure didn't move, didn't make a sound. Phosa took a cautious step forward; the torch held aloft like a beacon cutting through the shadows.

"Rusticus, it's me. Phosa." Her voice was softer this time, an attempt to coax him out of hiding.

With painstaking slowness, the figure rose from his crouched position, the hood falling back to reveal his face. His eyes, once loyal and warm, now held a glint of malice that chilled Phosa to her core.

"Phosa…" His voice resembled an animalistic groan. The fire had clearly changed more than just his face. She thought that even in the dark she could see a twisted smile playing on his partially blackened lips.

"What are you…?" Before Phosa could finish her sentence, Rusticus lunged forward, the torch falling from her grasp as she stumbled backward. In a flash, he was gone and the room erupted in chaos as the flames caught on the tapestries lining the walls. She gazed senselessly at the flames, wanting desperately to act, to do something but her body was frozen. She fell to the ground in a pile of defeated flesh; her eyes stung with smoke, and her lungs were overwhelmed. "Phosa, get up!" The voice was not her own. It was coming from the doorway. It belonged to a man, a voice she knew. Rusticus? And then everything went dark.

When she opened her eyes, everything hurt. She immediately sat up and coughed, not seeing Sarah, who was sitting next to her with a bowl of water and some white linens.

"Mistress, not so fast. Slow! Slow!" Her gentle, cool hands cupped the back of her head and lowered her back onto her pillow. There was a blurred figure standing at the head of her bed, but she couldn't make out the face.

"How is she?" Simon, that's definitely Simon's voice.

"She will be ok, master. She just needs rest."

Phosa tried to focus her eyes, but she was treated to a stinging ache in the back of her eye as a result. A larger, stronger hand caressed her cheek and said something soothing to her, but she couldn't understand the words. She noticed that the room didn't smell. *I must not be in the same room.* She remembered the cool and smooth touch of her blankets. *I'm in my room. Rusticus. What happened?*

"Rust— Rust—" Phosa desperately tried to get the words out.

"No, no, my darling, you must rest. Shh. Save your breath." He leaned his face in, close to hers, and the worry and love there came into focus.

"You must stay with her all night, Sarah."

"Yes, Lord."

"Phosa, get some rest and I'll have my father call in a doctor for you in the morning."

"Rust— Rust— Rusticus!" She tried one more time.

"Rusticus? Isn't that the name of your servant who—" Phosa only nodded.

"What about him?"

"Hhheee...is-"

"yes, he's what?"

"Here". All the strength in her body left in one instant, and Simon's face drifted off into a dark blur. And then there was nothing.

Striking pain woke her. It was dark. And she could hear the distant clang and chim of metal rims and carts as they pounded down Wanderer's Way. She knew she couldn't sleep any longer. The pain in her back was severe, but she did have her full vision back.

Fierce arguing erupted in the streets, and a chorus of barking dogs sounded in response. Fear gripped her again, as she imagined the scarred face of her former servant standing in the middle of the street, waiting for her to emerge. Phosa prayed silently for window shutters, pulling the blankets over her head.

Her eyes gently closed. Sleep approached and then retreated at the touch of cool metal upon her neck.

"You scream, you die." A menacing female voice spoke into the darkness. She bravely opened her eyes and was surprised to see the familiar olive complexion of her sweet handmaiden, Sarah.

Phosa lay frozen, her heart pounding in her chest as she stared at Sarah in confusion. The handmaiden's usually kind eyes were stern and unyielding, the flickering candlelight casting eerie shadows on her face. Phosa tried to calm her racing thoughts.

"What do you want?" Phosa managed to whisper, her voice barely above a strained breath.

Sarah leaned in closer. "You know too much, mistress." Sarah pressed the blade tighter to her throat, blocking Phosa's airway. She closed her eyes to avoid the pure hatred she saw in Sarai's brown eyes.

"You've been poking your nose where it does not belong," she hissed through clenched teeth.

"I....I don't" Phosa tried to speak through her squished airway.

"You don't what, donkey worshipper?" *Donkey worshiper? Is that what they're calling us now?*

Indignant, Phosa raised her body to meet the intruder's fearsome face.

"I don't know what you're talking about!"

Seemingly intimidated by Phosa's newfound bravery, Sarah released the dagger's pressure.

"Perhaps, but we will take you nonetheless."

"Take me? What? Where? What are you.... ?" Suddenly four men came out of the shadows of her bed chamber. She noticed one man dragging a heavy wooden club behind him, and another came at her quickly and forced a dark piece of cloth over her head. The knowledge of the club did nothing to ready herself for the blow. Then what light she could see through the cloth, faded entirely.

chapter twenty-two

COOL METAL

Phosa slowly opened her eyes and felt a persistent pounding pain behind her right eye, along with a sharp pain in her temple where the club had made contact. She raised her hands to touch her wound and found that her hands were bound in front of her.

She tried to control the urge to vomit on the bare, rough floorboards beneath her. *Where am I?* She thought to herself as she tried desperately to see out the black cloth that was still covering her face. She instinctively raised her hands to try and relieve herself of it, but it was no use. Her hands were rendered unusable, tied tightly in front of her. The incessant squeals of the cartwheels as it turned corners and climbed intersection barricades blended into the nightly roaming chorus sung in the streets of Rome.

The wooden floor was wet and stank of urine. She sensed movement and could hear the familiar shouts of drunken patrons of public houses, which were amongst the only establishments still open into the night. The cart was steered by a large muscular man with long dark hair and no cape. He stank of sheep dung.

Phosa sat up. Her hands were tied loosely with rope, and she carefully looked around to see if anyone was following them. Where did the rest of them go? She was sure there were at least four of them in her room. Laying back down, a tear escaped her still-pounding eyes. *Lord, find me. I need you.*

The troubled cart crossed the southern gate of Rome, and all that Phosa could see were the multitude of tombs lining the city's outskirts. *Lord am I coming to you?* Her heart moaned within her, feeling the end was near and she would need a marble slab tribute soon enough. The cart hobbled along the road and then came to an abrupt stop. She looked around and saw nothing but sparsely planted trees and the distant lights of the city.

This is it. This is where they'll find my body!

The man driving the cart jumped down from his perched seat at the head of the cart and roughly motioned for her to get out. She felt the man's tight grip on her arm, pushing her forward through the darkness. His maltreatment sent further threats of vomitous eruptions through her diaphragm, invading her throat. Fearing the repercussions of such an outburst, she swallowed it back, casting an unsavory expression on her already rattled exterior.

As she was dragged from the cart, she thought of all the things that she wouldn't get to do in this life. Find a good man to marry, have six children, and live on a farm far away from the troubles of the city. Those dreams were lofty now, as her feet carried her to a place she did not want to go. Without thinking and with no shame, the depths of her being came undone with a lament, "Oh Jesus, protect me. You are my strength and shield. You are my hope and salvation."

"None of that girl!" The brute yelled, pushing her harshly. His force caught her off guard and launched her off of the road and into the nearby ditch. Her hands bound, she had no way of bracing her fall and landed directly on her hip. The pain was startling and then lasting. She felt battered, and beaten.

"Don't you know that's why you're in the ditch?" The man mocked. "Now Get up! You have an appointment with death."

Phosa did not have the strength to launch herself out of the ditch but sank into an indignant pool of mud, resolved to her fate. "I said get up, you worthless scab!" His brutality reared its head again, as he grabbed her arm and threw her onto the ground above the ditch. She landed forcefully, hitting her chin on the grating gravel of the road.

With cruel intentions, her face covering was pulled off, exposing her to the terror that stood before her. A wall of armed soldiers their bows strung, and arrows directed at her. Ready to be launched at a word. Phosa raised herself up with some difficulty, her hands still bound in front of her. Her entire body shook with fear. She had seconds to decide if she would take this death, the death of a Christian going to see her God, run or at least make a stand against these accusers. Feeling like a fly caught in a spider's web, she had little choice. She wanted to live.

"Wait, I, this has been a mistake. I am but a simple plebeian woman!" Even before those words escaped her, she felt a pain worse than all the savagery she had already experienced: guilt.

The distant sound of a woman's cackling laughter interrupted the scene. The soldiers standing in front of her did not react, only smoothly stepped aside for a very small framed woman holding a torch. The light revealed a conniving smirk and determined dark blue eyes, that looked almost purple against the torchlight, like a lioness on the hunt. *Those eyes look so familiar.*

Phosa thought to herself, as the woman whispered orders to her men. Phosa could tell she was a woman of great wealth by the fashionable way she tied her hair back, the lavishly ornamented light blue silk dress, and four gold bands clasped around her wrists. *Who are you?*

"You, Tryphosa, are no simple woman."

"I know you from somewhere!" She shouted, without thinking.

The woman only smirked, revealing a dark cunning. "You are correct, Christian. You and your sister so very kindly received me in your small beggared market stall. You didn't know it then, but that day, you made your confession and sealed your fate. You both did." The woman stepped closer to her and then began to pace back and forth in front of her men.

"Carius?"

"Oh darling, do use your manners. You are about to die, aren't you? My name is Carius Quintus Junas."

Oh God, we are all doomed! She thought, remembering all that they had said to Carius in the market stall that morning. There was no way she or her sister could escape now. Phosa's heart beat like a war drum in her chest. She didn't know what to do or even think anymore. She was completely overcome by fear.

"And don't worry. I've known all about your superstitions way before you confessed all to me! We go way back to when your father was still around. May the gods watch over his soul! What a man your father was!" The woman paused for a moment and dreamily looked into the distance past Phosa. *What is she talking about?* "But no more of that! You, my dear, are doomed. I know all! Arsonists. Atheists. Traitors to Rome. Murderess and, worst of all, Christian!"

"And you had so much possibility, being educated! Even a plebeian can rise from the dirt if highly educated like yourself. But you threw it all away for what?" The woman didn't seem to care for an answer, and Phosa didn't want to give her one either.

"What would your father think, huh? He who valued you higher than even your older sister, teaching you to read and write like you are nobility! I'd love to know why he would do such a thing— But alas, we have no time for the story of poor, lonely, homeless orphans! I do take pity on you! Or at least I would if you were not a criminal! Arson is amongst the greatest crimes against Rome! But being a follower of the Way is the worst crime of all"

"I am no arsonist!"

"You and your sister burned down your insula, and left your servant to die!" Phosa felt the remains of her dinner threaten to reappear, as this strange woman recounted her deeds.

"But for what purpose?" She continued, the hatred dripping from her every word. "No one can know the reasoning of one who follows The Way! A superstition based on a donkey on a cross! How repulsive!"

"You know nothing about...."

"Oh but I do, and I know someone who knows even more. Rusticus? Come forward!" Out of the shadows, a dark figure emerged, his back twisted and sunken, his face a protruding menacing scowl. He appeared as an evil apparition, directly from her nightmares. His eyes were bloodshot, and the gruesome scar on the side of his face oozed as if it had never properly healed. He walked forward and stood next to Carius, whom Phosa guessed had hired him for some evil scheme.

For a brief moment, Rusticus raised his monstrous face and looked boldly into her soul. She could not hold his gaze, but instead leaned over the side of the road and vomited.

"This fellow wants to spill your blood." Carius declared, casually gripping Rusticus' shoulders. "And your sister's blood too. And who would blame him?"

The stench of vomit still lingered in her nostrils, mixing with the metallic scent of fear that emanated from her body.

"You and your sister must pay for your crimes, for every discoloration of my skin. For every jagged line! And for all the decades of pain!" Even in the dark of night, Phosa could see the anguish in his distorted eyes, and the venomous hatred that he must have hidden for her whole life. Suddenly, he rushed at her. His still-powerful arm clutched her throat and squeezed without mercy.

"You've ruined what dignity I did have, as a servant of superstitious donkey worshipers! Worshipers of a criminal and slave! How dare you reject our gods! The gods of your ancestors!" Phosa's face turned red, then pale as her eyes widened in terror. Her hands reached out, grasping at the empty air as if searching for a lifeline.

"Rusticus that's enough. Release her. We have a much worse fate planned for her."

Phosa inhaled a lungful of the salty and sour stench filling the air and collapsed onto the ground. She could still feel his fingers wrapped tightly around her neck. Rusticus obediently retreated into the darkness behind the woman.

"Listen to me girl, if you will recant your beliefs and rejoin proper Roman society, I will release you."

"Recant, and this will be a jovial story one day. And if not...the lions shall open their mouths!" Carius motioned for her force to step forward, their arrows now within two inches of Phosa's body.

"I am a Roman citizen! I demand a trial!"

"Oh, this is your trial! Unless you speak your allegiance to Jupiter now, and present your certification of sacrifice by the next full moon."

Phosa's gaze turned towards the sky and she saw that a half-moon twinkled back at her. Dismayed by her own weakness, she shook her head and faced her foes. She knew she could not think of cooperating with these people or denying her faith. *No! I'll never be a pagan again!* "You can do what you want with me! I'll make no sacrifice. I worship the one true God."

Carius' venomous glare compounded into a desperate lunge towards Phosa. Her hand slapped Phosa's delicate face, leaving flaming redness in its wake. "Quite the show! We'll see if your god will rescue you from the arena. Take her away!"

The waking sun rose over the violet-light blue horizon, a vision of hope, but none was felt. The silent procession walked a mile down the Via Tiburtina and veered off the road into what appeared to be a field. Tryphosa neither had the courage nor desire to know where she was going. She knew all roads led to death. She closed her eyes, thinking of the people that she loved, whom she would never see again. Even though theirs was a difficult relationship, she still loved her sister. And then, for the first time in a while, she allowed herself to think of Simon.

Her first love. Her only love. She could hear the slow caress of his voice as he whispered her name and feel the tantalizing thrill of his lips on hers.

The scratchy rope around her wrists burned her as she was pulled along through the open field. She looked around and saw nothing in front of her. The sun continued to peak over the hills, and in the distance, she could hear the gate to the city opening. Thinking of the city, she could not scale the great chasm that lay between her current terror and the life she once led. *OK, Phosa! No more of that! Remember what Peter said. Stand firm in your faith. Stand firm. Endure to the end.* She repeated Peter's words again and again until the great weight on her shoulders was released. A smile of peace spread across her face, and her wrists felt smooth and cool. All at once, her tired and battered body felt refreshed, as if she had just plunged into a cool spring.

"Thank you!"

"Ha! What are you thankful for? Prisoner!"

With joy she could not contain, she spoke with boldness, "My God has given me peace, which you don't understand, but with all my heart I pray that my death will show you the truth."

The woman who held her captive abruptly halted and spun around, her expression menacing. "Don't even bother trying to convert me to your superstitions."

"Your gods do not deserve your devotion."

"What of your God? He has not come down to rescue you, has He? And He will not! I and my company will be the last of the living that you will see."

Phosa was unsure whether to be relieved or dismayed when she asked, "Didn't you say my fate was to die in the arena?"

"I've changed my mind. I see now you are not only a murderous arsonist but a part of the pestilence that spreads your filthy superstition to the people of Rome. And Nero does not suffer your type to live long." She glanced over at the scarred face of her former servant only to see gratification.

"Jesus, claim my spirit." The words escaped her lips just as the party halted in front of a small marble structure. It had four engraved columns, a stone terrace, and three stairs leading to a set of double doors towering over it like a pair of heavenly guards.

"What is this place?" Phosa asked no one in particular.

Carius walked up the steps and studied the engravings of the columns silently. Her cold, sharpened face turned to that of a reverent follower. "This engraving warns of the retribution of the gods. I am honored to be their vessel."

Not feeling like her question had been answered, she asked again. to detach altogether from her body as it was pulled, yet again, into the darkness. Carius motioned for the large, muscular man to apprehend her again.

"You speak far too freely for your own good. But I will tell you nonetheless. This is the tomb of the unnamed. Your eternal home."

The doors were opened, and a retched waft of damp air mixed with excrement and decay escaped the tomb. The morning sun tried in vain to pierce the darkness inside, but it was rejected firmly.

"Down!"

Tired of being pulled all night, her frail arm threatened to detach altogether from her body as it was pulled, yet again, into the darkness. Then suddenly, Phosa thought she heard the sound of a horse galloping hard towards them. "Wait!" A young man's voice reverberated against the outer wall of the tomb. She turned and wondered if she was dreaming. She saw five men galloping hard towards them and a detachment of at least twenty foot soldiers behind.

She was sure her eyes deceived her, yet the group neared the tomb. The young man leading stopped his horse just short of Carius's wall of men and jumped off his horse. The young man wore the traditional armor of a Roman soldier and had a noble bearing. Then surprise took over. It was Simon. She was sure of it. Her mysterious savior had the same eyes and bearing as her almost lover.

"Carius Quintus Junas, you do not have jurisdiction here," Simon announced.

"Who you do you think you are, coming out here like this, and with such a mob?"

"I am Centurion Gaius Crassis Horitia." He answered, handing her a sealed parchment.

Phosa's eyes widened in horror. *Oh, dear God, he's impersonating a soldier!* With all her soul, she wanted to yell out to him that it was not worth risking his own life. She wanted to tell him to run, but she'd only reveal his true identity. Rusticus stood between his mistress and the soldier on horseback, his face clearly agitated. "My lady, surely we cannot let this nobody interrupt this criminal's sentence."

"Silence! He bears the seal of the praefectus."

Carius opened it and passed it back to Simon. "Read it!"

BY ORDER OF QUNARIUS HONORICUS CASSIAS, PRAEFECTUS URBI,

ALL PUBLIC PROSECUTION OF THOSE BEING ARRESTED FOR BEING PART OF THE NEW SUPERSTITION KNOWN AS THE WAY, ARE TO BE HANDLED DIRECTLY AND SOLELY BY THE COHORTES URBANE,

AS DEEMED ESTEEMABLE BY THE HIGHLY CULTIVATED AND ALTOGETHER MIGHTY EMPEROR NERO.

Carius let out a shrill shriek and then composed herself. "Very well, Centurion." Carius signaled for her men to step back. "The girl is yours. She is a criminal. Do your duty."

Simon roughly grabbed her by the arm and led her towards his steed, the rope that bound her still in his hands. Simon, an excellent actor, gave away nothing of his true self as he lifted himself up with ease and motioned his horse to start walking towards the city gate.

With the night's stress finally released, Phosa couldn't hold back her tears of relief. He saved her from certain death. Completely overwhelmed by the risk that he had taken, she knew that her heart would always be his. Tomorrow would be a different day full of love and devotion, no matter what disaster might follow them into the city.

The city gate loomed in front of them, guarded by dozens of soldiers on top of the walls and even more at the gate. The company suddenly came to a stop. Simon turned back and signaled for his men to inspect their bags and collect the toll that was required. He got off his horse and approached the three men on horseback behind her, pretending to have a discussion with them.

"Phosa, we are all in great danger," he said urgently.

Her mouth felt dry as she tried to swallow the lump in her throat. The fear and worry made her mouth taste bitter, like bile rising in her throat.

"Your sister...she's..."

"What? What happened to Phena?" she interrupted.

"Phosa, your sisters been taken. She's in Nero's hands now."

THE END

STELLA	A stella refers to a stone or wooden monument, often inscribed with writing
STOLA	A stola was a traditional garment worn by women in ancient Rome,
STRATA	road or street
STULTISSIME!	Complete idiot!
SUBLIGAR	essentially a loincloth or a pair of shorts
TABLINUM	office
THERMOPOLIUM	A Roman establishment that served hot food and beverages
TISANA BARRICA	a type of herbal tea or infusion
TUTULUS.	was a type of head covering or hat worn in ancient Rome, particularly by women.
VAPULABIS	Latin phrase: 'you will be flogged!"

PLEASE LEAVE A REVIEW OF

Seven Hills One Light

Would you consider taking two minutes of your time and leaving an honest review on Amazon? Just search my title, click on the book listing and scroll down until you see

"Write a Review for this Product"

OR

about the
AUTHOR

HAZEL DAINS is a Canadian debut novelist whose love for ancient history and science fiction fuels her writing. Her extensive travels, particularly through Italy, shaped the richly detailed worlds in her historical fiction, while her fascination with futuristic possibilities breathes life into her science fiction tales. When Hazel isn't researching ancient civilizations or envisioning distant worlds, she's enjoying quirky hobbies like baking intricate historical desserts or curating her antique map collection. From epic pasts to speculative futures, Hazel's stories are bound to captivate. Watch for her exciting sequel, *"Seven Trials One Exodus"* and more adventures in science fiction.

For free books, sequel sneak peaks and to find out what's coming next,

FOLLOW HAZEL:

@HAZELDAINSWRITES

www.hazeldains.com